JILLIAN HART

CHAPTER ONE

Montana Territory—1864

Night deepened as Garnet Jones climbed off the stagecoach and studied what she could see of the dark mining town. There wasn't much. Small campfires glowed like embers on a flat expanse of ground. On the other side of the street the many windows of saloons and brothels lit up the darkness.

Garnet heard a gunshot explode inside one of the buildings. A woman screamed. A man shouted.

"I'm scared," fifteen-year-old Golda whispered, clinging to the side of the stagecoach. "Maybe we shouldn't have come."

"We had no choice." Garnet thought of Pa and the letter she'd received. The man had fathered her and she had a duty to him, no matter how tempting turning back may be.

"Welcome to Stinking Creek, ma'am," the stagecoach driver announced. He threw down their few bags. The valises hit the ground with a muffled thunk, kicking up thick plumes of dust. "This here's the end of the line."

Well, they were in the right town, but it wasn't an impressive place. Or a particularly nice-smelling one. Garnet wrinkled her nose, staring briefly at a dirty, obviously drunk miner doing his personal business on the walkway between the brothel and the saloon. "Don't look, Golda."

Golda snapped her head so fast, she nearly lost her balance in order to stare in amazement and perhaps curiosity at the indecent sight.

"I said, don't look," Garnet instructed, her indignation growing with each shaky breath. The golden glow from the well-lit tavern glinted through the large window, illuminating him clearly. He had the audacity to tip his hat to her, his business now done, before striding back into the saloon to liquor himself up further.

"I know why they call it Stinking Creek." Garnet shook her head. This was just the sort of place she should have expected. Some derelict mining camp without a bit of civilization.

Perhaps Golda was right. Perhaps they shouldn't have come. Perhaps they should have sent a communication from Virginia City instead.

"Struck gold here last summer. Not a good strike, mind ya. And it ain't the safest camp around." The stooped, foul-smelling driver stepped closer and picked up their few bags. He wheezed when he spoke. "A man was murdered a while back. Are you sure you wanna stay, ma'am? Only the workin' kinda girls come to this town. I don't think we've had no quality ladies like yerselves here before. Unless you two, uh, are looking to, uh, find employment."

"We're staying, and not to find work." Garnet clucked her tongue as she gave the little man a hard look. Certainly he wasn't suggesting she was a soiled dove. Appalled by the mere thought of it, she snatched Golda's bags from his despicable grip and shoved them into her younger sister's arms.

"I ken take you girls back to Virginia City. This ain't no place for the likes of you." The driver spat a stream of foul brown juice into the dirt at his feet. He bent stiffly to lift up her valise, but Garnet was quicker.

She snatched the sturdy handles firmly before he could toss her belongings back aboard. She was staying, whether she liked it or not. "This is hardly my idea of paradise, but that can't be helped. I must find our pa. He's staying with a Mr. Tanner. Do you know him?"

The driver stood, thinking deeply. Using his brain was clearly an effort. The glow from the tavern's window brushed the driver's face with orange and black shadows while he ruminated. "Tanner? He lives just out that-a-way." He pointed an age-crooked finger away from town, where the dark shades and shadows of night beckoned.

"Do you know how far?"

"Not too far. Keeps to himself, though. Ain't the social type." The driver spat again. "I don't reckon a nice gal like you wants to see Wyatt Tanner."

"Why not?" Garnet felt a chill prickle at the nape of her neck.

"Folks say he's dangerous."

"Dangerous?"

"Deadly." The driver shivered as if he were afraid, too. "Well, I gotta get going, missy. You gals take care of yerselves."

Golda gasped, and her fingers gripped Garnet's arm with a panicked clench. "Did you hear what he said? A man was murdered. We're not safe here. Oh, we never should have come."

"You're the one who didn't want to leave Pa here by himself. And since we're here, we'd best not panic," Garnet replied, sensibly. "You know we can't up and abandon Pa now, not after we've traveled so far."

"I guess not." Golda sighed heavily. "But I'm still frightened."

Truth be told, so was Garnet.

The stagecoach rolled away, spewing up black clouds of dust into the air like fog. Garnet coughed, quickly covering her face with a handkerchief. The dust stuck in her throat so she could hardly breathe. But that wasn't the worst of her problems. Not by a long shot. They were alone in the middle of the night in a disreputable mining camp looking for a dangerous man. Another term of school teaching was a more inviting prospect than this.

"What do we do now?" Golda's voice wobbled.

"We find a hotel room for the night."

"Do you think they have a nice hotel in a place like this?" Golda choked on a little sob.

Garnet gazed about the sorry excuse for a town. The moonless sky left the faces of the buildings in shadows as she stood, eyes adjusting to the darkness. Fear shivered down her spine, but she shrugged it away. She hadn't traveled all this way to be frightened. She had a job to do, and, by golly, nothing would stop her.

"Come." She took hold of Golda's gloved hand. "Maybe there's a better place down the block."

"But it's so dark."

It was dark, but the buildings lining the streets were lighted and, from the look of it, filled to capacity. She could hear the shouts of men in the saloons, the jeering argument over a card game, and the tinny piano music filtering out into the street like lamplight.

This was not a decent town.

Perhaps she had best rethink her plan. She had not expected the West to be quite so . . . rough.

"I see you're just off the stage," a woman's friendly voice called out. "You girls looking for work?"

"What kind of work?" Oh. Garnet remembered the stage driver's words. "No, I guess we aren't working girls."

"Too bad. We could use more help. It's real busy this time of year."

Garnet stared at the woman, who posed in a lighted doorway of what could only be a brothel. Goodness, she'd never held a conversation with a prostitute before. Then again, ever since she'd left Willow Hollow, nothing had been the same.

"Are you girls lost?" the soiled dove asked, ever helpful. "Speak up, so's I can help you out. This ain't no town where a body should be standing around on the street."

Before Garnet could answer, a gunshot exploded from somewhere inside one of the saloons. A horrible, hairsplitting whiz buzzed past Garnet's head and a bullet lodged into the wooden wall of a trough not two feet away. Water spilled through the bullet hole, running out onto the dry, dusty earth.

Garnet stared at the stream of water winking in the small bit of light from the open brothel door. Her knees knocked. She didn't like this town. Not one little bit. "We're, ah, looking for a hotel."

"A hotel? There ain't anything like that here." The woman chuckled. "Did you girls take the wrong stage?"

"I wish we had." Garnet glanced up and down the street, wondering when the next bullet might split the air. Or knock them both to the ground dead. "Maybe you could help us. I'm looking for Mr. Wyatt Tanner. He has been kind enough to look after my ill father, and I've come to retrieve him."

"Ah." The soiled dove nodded. "Wyatt is a . . ."

"A dangerous man?" Garnet supplied.

"Yes." The woman shrugged, a simple gesture. "Wyatt doesn't like people. It might be best if you girls waited until morning to hunt him down. Perhaps we could find you a room for the night. Maybe something . . ." she hesitated.

"Respectable?" Garnet offered.

"I'll try."

"I'd rather just find Pa," Golda said quietly. Her voice quaked in fear. "I worry he's dead by now. That we've arrived too late."

Garnet closed her eyes. She was tired, afraid, and did not want to stand out on this street any longer. She feared more than bullets. Who knew what type of men frequented that saloon, gambled and . . . *recreated* in those buildings? If she breathed deeply she could smell the horrible condition of the town—the result of too many men living on their own without a woman's firm guidance and good judgment. Dear Lord, didn't men have enough sense in their big heads to know how to sweep and wash and bathe?

"Well, if you would rather, Wyatt's cabin is the last at the end of town." The woman said Mr. Tanner's given name as if she knew him well. As if she . . . Garnet didn't complete that thought.

"The last cabin, you say?"

"Yes. Just walk that-a-way toward the mountains, and you can't miss it."

"Thank you," Garnet said cordially and turned. Hitching her skirts high, she carefully stepped over several tobacco juice stains left by the stagecoach driver and the round, telltale wet patch beside the saloon.

"Suppose it isn't safe to be walking down these streets," Golda whispered, standing frozen with fear in the dusty road. "Especially in the dark."

Several gunshots rang out inside one of the buildings, and Garnet winced. No bullets buzzed past her, but she didn't feel safe. Through an uncovered window, she could see the inside of one of the many saloons. A woman dressed in red with her bosom showing danced on the top of a table. The men's hoots and jeers resounded in the cool night air.

This was simply not a surprise. Leave it to their pa, weak in morals, to end up in a despicable camp such as this. She doubted if there was even a church in town. Well, there was simply no alternative. They could not stand about on the street all night waiting for the next whizzing bullet. Garnet grabbed her sister by the arm and tugged. They started down the street.

"What if we can't find Pa after all?" Golda whispered. "What if he's already gone? What if we've come all this way for nothing?"

"Pa had better still be alive," Garnet bit out harshly enough so she didn't sound quite so afraid. "The hardship that man has placed upon this family is a disgrace. If he isn't dead, then he had better start praying. When I catch up to him, I'll—"

"Garnet," Golda hissed. "Look. Someone's coming toward us."

A shadow moved up ahead on the darker part of the street where no buildings stood. There was little light to make out what moved there, but from the sound of the footfalls, Garnet didn't need to wonder. She knew. Another irresponsible man who would rather cause trouble, break the law, or play with his guns and his patch of dirt than hold a respectable job. The town was probably packed with vile men just like him.

"Howdy girls," he called out, rough and deep, and he changed his direction just to intercept them. "Are ya havin' a slow night?"

Garnet stared at the man, deeply repulsed at his friendliness. Goodness, they were decent women. He was dressed so darkly she could hardly make him out except for the flash of guns strapped to both thighs. The sight made her heart quake.

He strolled closer, his chuckle deep as he called out, "How much'll it cost me fer both of ya?"

Golda whimpered, and Garnet skidded to a halt. Cost him? For what? Indignation rolled over her, stealing away some of her fear. He thought they were selling their charms on the street. Why, she'd simply never been mistaken for a . . . heavens, she had never been so insulted.

"I said, how much?"

"How much?" Garnet hissed. "A decent woman is worth more than you can pay."

"Is that so?" The man cocked one eyebrow, interested now. "I got me a lot of gold."

"A lot of gold?" Oh, she was mad. "Is that all?"

"Ain't that enough?"

Garnet thought of how Pa had left them over the years. "A woman wants much more than a bit of silly dust. She requires substance of character and steadfast integrity. Both of which you obviously lack."

She glared at the sorry excuse for a man. It was evident he had no moral fiber. He'd probably abandoned a wife and half a dozen children just to hunt for gold in the wilderness.

Just like her pa had.

Deplorable. Simply deplorable. She had no notion what the world was coming to.

The man blushed furiously and ran off in the night.

A lot of gold indeed! Garnet huffed. No wonder Pa had found his way here. He was among his kind—shiftless men who dreamed of achieving fortunes without an honest day's labor. She was greatly displeased to see for herself the depth to which civilization would sink without a woman's firm hand. Surely they could locate Pa, board him on the next stage out of town, and be away from this foul camp.

If she could survive the smell.

CHAPTER TWO

Wyatt Tanner had a headache that drilled through his left temple at an angle behind his eye and bored right through the back of his head. Then it ricocheted like a bullet in a barrel. Darn cheap whiskey. It did this to him every time.

He should have skipped the poker tables tonight. It was Saturday, almost Sunday morning. A time when all thoughts turned to home. Some drank to forget, while others drank to console themselves, missing the womenfolk they'd left behind. It was all they moaned about as they made their bets and played their hands.

In all, it was a grim night and not good for his kind of business, listening to the talk that came when liquor loosened tongues. He wasn't going to find out any more information, not by playing poker with men who would think of nothing else but the women they left on purpose.

Yep, good thing he was heading home for a good night's sleep. He'd have better luck tomorrow. Wyatt pulled the brim of his hat low over his eyes and kept walking.

The slightest noise crackled behind him on the dark, desolate road.

He froze, his senses alert. His heart pounded triple time. He thought of the killer he'd come here to find and of the substantial gold he'd won at the tables tonight. Both made him a target for a murderer. Taking no chances, his fingers inched toward his holsters.

There it was again. Sounded like a double pair of footsteps coming from town. He squinted into the darkness, but he hadn't been outside long enough for his eyesight to adjust to the moonless night.

The entire population of Stinking Creek was in town gambling and drinking. These men, they had to be following him. Until he solved the murders in this town, Wyatt would take no chances. He headed for cover and drew his revolver.

The two figures moved closer. He squatted down beside a skinny tree trunk. Two short men. He could see the movements of their hats against the background of leaves and branches. They moved closer, slow and cautious, oblivious to the target they made. Then he heard it, the sound of voices high and quarreling.

Those were no men. Not with those swishing petticoats. Why in the devil's clutches were two women squawking like a flock of hens on his road? Worse, they were paying no attention to their surroundings. They did not notice the dark figure looming behind them in the pitch-black night.

Wyatt watched as the man drew a rifle. The barrel shone black as the midnight rider aimed at one of the women. Wyatt didn't hesitate. He pulled the trigger, his pistol fired, and a woman screamed.

Heart pounding, he broke out of the underbrush and into a run down the path, his gaze trained on the last movement of the horse and rider. But there was only shadows and forest.

Where did he go? Wyatt knew he'd hit the man; he had no doubt. Maybe it was a thief. Or maybe it was the killer he was hunting.

Wyatt drew up short when he spotted something up ahead. It was a rifle, left on the road. He knelt down to examine it, his senses alert to any danger he couldn't see. The stock felt wet. He examined it. Wet with blood.

He wanted to chase down the shooter, but his conscience reminded him of the women in the road, defenseless and probably terrified. They needed his help, whoever they were. Beneath the plain miner's garb beat the heart of a deputy marshal. His first concern was to make certain the women were unharmed and helped to safety.

Then he would get back to the job of hunting down his brother's killer.

He retrieved his lantern from the side of the road and lit it. Orange flames licked to life as he approached the fallen women. His heart stammered at the sight of the single female form sprawled on the ground. Light flickered across her still body.

"Where did the other girl go?" He lifted the lantern and light spilled across the road. He could easily see the bent stalks of bunchgrass and shivering leaves.

"You don't have to be afraid," he called. "I won't hurt you."

No answer. Well, he would worry about the one who couldn't run off, the one unconscious at his feet. He shifted the lantern, shadows dancing over her still form.

She was no fresh-faced maiden, not with those fine creases around her full mouth and lines in the corners of her closed eyes. But she was no hard-bitten woman either. Wyatt could see the softness of her skin, pearl-smooth even in this rough light.

She wore a modest gray dress, a fabric without print or stripes or tiny flowers. The material stretching across her small breasts and tightly cinched waist was plain and unadorned. Her full skirt had ballooned up under her, perhaps as a result of her fall, to reveal white pantaloons and socks. A bright stain grew in the muslin covering her upper thigh. Blood. She'd been shot.

He knelt down to study the rent fabric and skin. The small bullet hole revealed a raw tear and several layers of opened flesh. She'd only been nicked by the bullet, for it looked like a superficial wound. Wyatt shook his head, relieved. She was lucky and he was damn grateful, since there wasn't a doctor brave enough to set up practice in the notoriously rough mining camp of Stinking Creek.

Now that he knew she wasn't dead or dying, great questions troubled him. Who was she? Where did she come from? And most importantly, why? He didn't recognize her face. She certainly wasn't one of the town's painted ladies.

He eased the knife from his pocket and glanced around, watching the shiver of the shadowed trees in the slight wind. An owl glided by on outstretched wings. He heard no human sounds.

He exposed the sharp knife's blade. Its steely edge caught the thin lantern light and flashed in the darkness. He was no doctor, but he would do what he could. Even if it wasn't safe here kneeling in the road. Listening for the return of the dark rider, he reached for a length of the woman's starched petticoats and sliced off a good bit of hem.

The sound of fabric tearing blended with the other sounds of night. The chirp of insects, the hoot of an owl, the call of a wolf in the distance. A closer one answered. Wyatt considered the direction of the wind. Would the wolves smell blood and move in?

He quickly tied the band of cloth tight about the wound. Immediately blood began to seep through the bandage. Wyatt studied that growing stain, bright crimson against snowy white muslin. He'd best get her to shelter. His cabin was the nearest place.

Well, it looked like he was saddled with another patient to look after, whether he wanted her or not. He was no darn nurse. He had a murder to solve and a life of his own to get back to. Stinking Creek wasn't his idea of paradise.

Another wolf's cry sliced through the night. They had no time to dally. Wyatt wondered where the second woman had disappeared to. She'd probably run to hide from him. There was no way she could know he wasn't a threat. He listened for the sound of her in the woods, but heard only the movement of animals scurrying for cover. The wolves were here.

He tucked his left arm beneath the woman's knees and his right beneath her shoulders. He could feel the curve of her ribs and the rounding of her bottom. All female. Her head bobbed from side to side, then gently rolled to rest against his shoulder. Her lustrous dark hair felt like black silk against his chin. He tried not to pay attention, tried not to remember the last time he held a woman, his wife. His chest ached. Yes, best not to think of that.

It wasn't a long walk back to his cabin, but the night wrapped silently around him. He sensed the dark, shadowy presence of the wolves. Wyatt walked faster, always aware of the woman in his arms.

* * *

Golda Jones bit back the hard cold ball of fear in her chest. She crouched behind a thick, dark patch of tree branches. She had been careful not to make even one sound. It was difficult. Small twigs littering the ground beneath her shoes threatened to snap beneath the slightest shift of her weight. Willowy branches caught in her hair and moved with each intake of breath.

The moment she realized their lives were in peril, Golda had run for the cover of the forest. She'd been halfway there when she realized Garnet had fallen. Torn by indecision, she'd debated what to do. But when that gun-toting ruffian came dashing toward them, fear had overtaken loyalty and she'd hidden from the outlaw the best she could.

She just happened to have hold of both reticules, and she clutched them tightly to her belly. Garnet would want her to safeguard them, for all of their savings were tucked inside. If that outlaw took their gold, how else would they afford safe passage back home?

Although the villain carried a small lantern, she could not see enough of the road to tell if Garnet still lived. Now the man stepped into a soft glow of light. A cold hand of fear reached right out and clutched her rapidly beating heart. The dark stranger scanned the forest as if he knew she was there, as if he sensed her watching him. She snapped her eyes shut and stood in absolute darkness, terror pumping through her veins.

Golda opened her eyes. Far ahead in the oppressive night, she could see the man staggering under the weight of something he carried like a huge sack of grain. Garnet! She swallowed the scream in her too-dry throat. He was packing off her sister's body.

Her grief hammered through her in one cold sweep. Golda leaned her forehead against the reassuring solidity of the tree trunk. The bark was hard and rough against her fair skin. She held her breath until every urge to scream had faded.

Silence settled around her, as thick as fog. Funny, not even the wind seemed to blow.

The tiny hairs on the back of her neck rose, and Golda didn't need to turn around. She saw the slow movement low on the ground, a dark liquid blackness that shrank to absolute stillness when she looked at it.

Wolves.

Losing all rational thought, she screamed. Her cry rose up in the night, rending the thick silence that had settled over the earth like a warm wool blanket. With her heart in her throat, she grabbed tight hold of her skirts and ran. The dark shadows followed her, then sprang to life.

This time she didn't scream. She didn't have the chance.

* * *

Garnet knew she was dead. Yes, she was certain of it. First, there was the complete and utter weightlessness of her body. Second, there was the absolute blackness that met her eyes when she opened them.

Heaven wasn't what she expected. Light, maybe. Angels, certainly. But not this sense of aloneness. Or pain. Sheets of it, sharp and biting, right in the middle of her thigh. Her entire body tightened against the torture. She clenched her jaw until her teeth hurt. She tried to draw air into her constricted lungs and realized that since she was breathing, she must not be dead after all.

One thing was for certain. She wasn't lying in the dusty path where she last remembered being. There was no smell of that powder-dry earth, no sound of a wild breeze through leafy trees, no night animals moving in the shadows. She smelled day-old greasy cooking and coffee grounds. Oh, and something that smelled rather . . . well, bad.

Garnet sniffed again. It was the scratchy blanket that covered her—an unwashed blanket. Realization skittered over her. She remembered walking along the worn path with Golda, heatedly discussing how tired they were, how afraid they would be of Mr. Wyatt Tanner when they found him, and how they feared Pa already dead.

She remembered the shots ringing out like a thunderclap in the night. She hadn't realized she'd been hit, then her leg had buckled beneath her and she'd pitched face-forward into the dirt. There hadn't been pain then, only a cold wave of recognition that she'd been shot, washing over her with the fury of a prairie cyclone.

She was in some cabin in Stinking Creek, Montana, that awful mining town, all of which could use a good washing.

She summoned the strength to toss the odoriferous blanket off her. She wished she knew how she'd gotten into this bed and who had placed her here.

"Golda?" she whispered into the darkness.

A man's single snore answered.

Well, Golda did not snore, so whoever it was sleeping over there in the darkness could not be her. That meant . . . yikes. She was alone in a cabin with a strange man. Was Golda missing? Or was she unconscious?

Garnet feared for her baby sister, the girl she'd practically raised since their mother's illness and then death. Garnet was a woman who took her responsibilities seriously. "Golda?"

Another low nasal snore.

She remembered a demon-man dashing out of a small grove of trees, but that was all. Panic pulsed through her chest. She had to calm herself. She had to think rationally. She'd learned in her twenty-six years of living that there was always a logical solution to any problem, great or small, if only one took the time to think about it.

Well, if her captor was sleeping so soundly, there was only one thing to do. Escape.

The bed ropes creaked when she shifted her weight. Garnet froze, waiting, but the snoring continued. Relief washed over her. She hadn't awakened her captor, so she dared to stand. A light-headed buzz fluttered through her head, but she fought it. A little dizziness wasn't going to stop her.

White-hot pain speared through her thigh each time she put weight on it. Garnet drew in a slow, steady stream of air, refusing to give up. She hadn't failed at anything before this, and she hadn't come all this way to Montana Territory to lose her freedom and her sister all in one night. What was a little pain when compared with one's life?

A gray light crept through the cracks around the door, guiding her way, and luckily the door was unlatched. It whispered open on leather straps, opening to the sounds of the night. Crickets and owls and wind. Freedom beckoned to her and, grateful her captor was a heavy sleeper, she took a step. The wood creaked beneath her feet as she limped across the threshold.

Stars peeked between scattering clouds, casting some light upon the earth. She could make out the line of majestic trees and the thin ribbon of the road. The snoring behind her continued, and, assured of her chances, she hobbled down the worn path.

"Going somewhere?" A man's mocking voice cut through the night.

Garnet's heart pounded with the fury of a chugging steam engine. It couldn't be. Her captor was snoring up a storm back in the cabin. She twisted around when she heard footsteps, just a couple, light and nearly weightless upon the earth.

Sweet heavens! The man stalking toward her was the same one who'd dashed out of the woods with a gun. Now she remembered there had been two men, one mounted on a big dark horse, another dashing out of the woods with a blazing gun.

"Where's my sister? What have you done with her?"

His silence infuriated her. "She's a mere child. Not even sixteen years old. If you've harmed her, I swear I'll . . . I'll . . . well, I don't know what I'll do, but I will make you pay."

He strode closer with the physical prowess of a hunting wolf. "A bullet might stop most men, but not you, I see."

"I'm tougher than I look," Garnet challenged, but the fine hairs at the base of her neck prickled. She heard nothing, no soft footfalls in the inches-thick dust, no whisper of clothing . . . but he advanced on her anyway. Powerful. Dangerous. Captivating.

She'd never seen a man with such broad shoulders. Not that she made it a habit to look at different anatomical parts of men's bodies. Heavens, she was a proper sort of woman and a schoolteacher to boot, but this man . . . why, he made her stomach flutter.

Ah, don't go dreaming again, Garnet reminded herself. No man thought she was worth a second look. She knew she was no beauty; certainly she'd heard that often enough back home, where all the broad-shouldered men crossed the street to avoid her and even the pasty, greasy-haired men ran in the opposite direction.

Their indifference hurt, but she'd gotten used to it. Men liked females who were pretty and simpering, things she could never be, no matter how hard she tried.

But Golda was and she needed protecting. And no fine pair of male shoulders should distract Garnet from her responsibilities. "Answer me. What did you do with my sister?"

"She ran for cover when you were shot. I haven't seen her."

"You just left her alone in the—"

"You were injured. You still are." His words whispered along the back of her neck. "I did go back to look for her."

"Did you find—"

"Just tracks." Low and deep, that voice. He towered over her, a powerful flesh-and-blood man, his shoulders wide and his feet planted firmly. "I went through your valises. I wanted to know who I was dealing with, what kind of woman would be wandering around in this town at night."

"You violated my privacy? You—"

"You were trespassing on my land." He had a rude habit of interrupting. With his hands braced on his narrow hips, he strolled around her and into the sweep of starlight. He was dressed simply, like all miners. He wore Levi's and a cotton shirt stretched over a muscle-hewn chest. "For all I knew, you were a danger to me with a loaded gun hidden in your satchel."

"Sorry," she breathed, "but I was—"

"Looking for Eugene, I know." He no longer looked threatening, but that dangerous handsome quality cloaked him like the night shadows. "You're the old maid who's come to fetch him home."

Garnet had never met this kind of man before, so powerful he took her breath away. He looked like the sort of man a sensible woman should never trust. Besides, he was far too busy looking at the sky, the trees, the grounds, the cabin. At everything but her. A common habit with men, for she wasn't pretty.

Even a low-life, devastatingly handsome outlaw didn't find her attractive.

Heart aching, she stared hard at the ground. "Do you know where my pa is? We've been so long in responding to Mr. Tanner's letter, he could be dead by now or—"

"I'm still taking care of him."

Garnet shivered, her gaze drifting upward. She couldn't help it. There was no mistaking the steel strength of the man. It rang in his voice and burned in his dark eyes. "Then where is Mr. Tanner?"

"I'm Wyatt Tanner."

"*You?*" This dangerous loner who looked more powerful than a bear? This was the man caring for Pa?

She was doomed.

"Surprised, huh?" Wyatt struck a match to light a cigar. A small tongue of flame chased away the dark then faded. He watched her step back from his presence hiding her mouth behind one hand. So prim and proper. Just the sort of woman he'd never understood, never felt comfortable around.

He puffed on his cigar, breathed deep, savored the smoke. Women. He'd never developed a good opinion of the creatures during his lifetime. The West wasn't populated by all that many civilized women, but the few he'd seen over the years were enough to give him indigestion Or break his heart.

Truth was, he hadn't expected old Eugene's daughter to show up at all. No sensible woman would make such a dangerous journey across uncivilized land just to rescue an old cheater of a father who didn't seem to miss his family one bit.

Still, it spoke well for the woman. Garnet Jones had more courage and loyalty than most he'd met.

"There's a stage leaving tomorrow. There will be another one in a week, if we're lucky."

"What do you mean?"

"The first snows could hit these mountains at any time. You could be stranded here." She was shot, and the old man wasn't strong enough to travel. But they had to leave tomorrow, no matter what.

The last thing he needed was more bodies crowding his cabin, crowding his life. He had a job to do. And a past he didn't want to face.

"I'm not about to spend the winter in a tiny cabin with an old man and his maiden daughters." He tried to sound kind. "You won't like it. I won't like it. I want you on tomorrow's stage, you understand?"

"Yes, but—"

Her set chin was perfectly visible, hoisted up a notch so that her face tipped up toward the sky. He could see the trembling of that chin, as if she clenched her teeth to still the shaking, but couldn't quite control it.

She was afraid. She was injured. She said she was Eugene's daughter. Heaven help him. "No buts. No arguments. You can't stay here after tomorrow."

"I have to." How stubborn she was. "I must find my sister."

"I tried. Likely as not she'll show up come morning safe and sound."

"What if she doesn't? Please, you have to help me. She's my littlest sister."

Wyatt tapped the ashes from the tip of his cigar. He tried not to look at the woman, but he couldn't help it. There was a vulnerability in her that called to him. She was helpless and injured, hurt because he hadn't been fast enough to stop the man following her, to keep him from firing. Unlike some women he knew, she was loyal to family. She'd come here to care for her father.

Family loyalty. It was a concept he hadn't known much of in his life. He'd only had his brother, and now . . . He stared down at his empty hands, unable fix all that had gone wrong. Ben was gone.

Wyatt Tanner, whether he liked it or not, was alone. Meant to be that way. Meant to stay that way.

CHAPTER THREE

Garnet turned toward the cabin and her courage ebbed. The structure wasn't far, but it felt like a thousand miles away. The thought of forcing her leg to carry her that far left her weak. Fear had driven her from the cabin, but now she didn't have quite enough to make up for the teeth-gnashing pain streaking through her thigh. She knew she might as well fly to the moon as hobble a few yards to that dark, stuffy cabin.

Well, Pa was in there, and the thought steadied her. Perhaps that was why she hadn't felt exactly alone in the cabin. He had been sleeping there, quiet and ill, in the dark where she couldn't have spotted him. "If I can't find Golda, then please let me see my pa."

His voice rose out of the darkness, blending with the shadows. "Your beloved father is sacked out in my cabin. I hate to say it, but I'm glad you're here. Now I can finally get rid of that"—he paused in the middle of criticizing her father—"of that gol darned—"

She couldn't believe her ears. Why didn't Mr. Tanner disparage her father? Could it be this tough man hid a polite nature?

She almost smiled. "You can call him whatever you want. I know Pa is—"

"A whining complainer of a man."

"You're being awfully polite. I would have used harsher words."

"What? I thought—"

"What? That I'm devoted to my pa?" Her good leg buckled and she slipped to her knees in the dust. The chalky smell of earth rose up to itch her nose, and she cried out as her injured leg slammed hard into the ground.

"You aren't?" Wyatt's fingers steeled around her elbow, helping her up.

"I'm honest when it comes to Pa." The iron strength of him vibrated through her. Her spine began to tremble, sending ripples of shivers through her limbs. But it wasn't from the pain. She'd never been this close to a man who wasn't a relative. Goodness, but it was a strange sensation. Warm tingles danced up her arm, fizzed in her blood.

"Here," he rumbled like thunder. "Lean on me."

His arm reached around her shoulders, rock-hard and immovable. He wouldn't let her fall, she knew. How had he gotten this strong? With every step, Garnet tried not to think of the way his iron-corded body moved against hers, so hard and hot she forgot all about her pain.

"That's right." Encouragement softened his rum-rich voice. "You don't have much farther to go."

Heavens, how could she think about something as mundane as walking when this distracting man was holding her tight? His touch burned like fire, his strong male presence chased all thought from her head. Something primal made her heartbeat drum thick and loud in her ears.

What was wrong with her? Had she lost so much blood that it was affecting her reasoning? What kind of woman did that make her? She had been able to resist all the men back home in Willow Hollow, but she felt tingly all over from the touch and closeness of this perfect stranger.

No matter how well-made the man, her primary concerns ought to be that her sister was missing and her father was ill.

"Men die of brain fever," she said now, trying hard to focus her mind away from this handsome, dangerous stranger and back on the pain in her leg. Yes, pain. That ought to make her think of something besides Wyatt Tanner's steely chest. "I can't thank you enough for all you've done. For saving Pa's life and mine. You knew nothing about me, yet you didn't leave me in the woods after I was shot."

"Well, I considered it, but truth was, I was afraid you would still be there come morning and scare my horse."

"So helping me was a convenience?" Oh, she saw right past his tough facade.

"Something like that. Watch the step up."

His protection washed over her like starlight. Garnet caught her toe on the step, and pain ricocheted through her injured leg.

His strong arms scooped her up against his chest before she knew what he was doing. How powerful he was! Goodness, she couldn't seem to breathe because her lungs felt so incredibly tight. A good percentage of her body was in direct contact with his, rock-hard and far too intimate. She could feel his every step, his every breath.

A part of her could not deny it was simply scandalous. A proper woman never allowed a man to carry her around like a . . . well, Garnet didn't know what. But another part of her felt dizzy, almost giddy. It was like flying, and all too soon it was over. He set her down on the hard, unpleasant-smelling bed. That blanket, that's what it was. It needed a decent washing.

It just went to show that no matter how kind and charismatic Mr. Wyatt Tanner was, he was not so different than her pa. He lived and worked the same way, with as little effort as possible. Even when it came to doing laundry.

"You've probably opened up that wound again. Just when I got the bleeding stopped. I'd better change that bandage." He moved in the darkness. She heard a clank of tin and the scrape of a drawer opening. "Let me find the matches, and with a little bit of light, I'll be able to see. There they are."

Garnet couldn't catch her breath as Wyatt set the lantern on the table near her elbow. Her body still tingled from his touch, her blood still circulated a strange heat through her veins.

He struck up a flame and lit the lantern's wick. Light danced to life, pushing away the darkness and nudging it back toward the shadowed corners, revealing the breadth and shape of the man towering over her. He reached into his pocket and withdrew a knife.

But it was the sight of him that drew her. All this time she'd not seen what he looked like with a lantern's glow caressing the side of his face, showing the darkness, as deep as the night, in his eyes. Illuminating the hard plane of his nose and the curve of his jaw, the high cheekbones that made his face rugged.

"You won't hurt me, will you?" Her words trembled when she spoke. "I can't imagine a man has much opportunity to hone his nursing skills."

"I managed before. Hold your breath."

So he had put the bandage on her thigh, the bandage that was now blood-soaked. Garnet nearly panicked until she saw the flash of humor in his eyes, eyes that were deep and full of secrets. She sensed Wyatt was a private man, a loner. Of course, he was a prospector. Like her father, he'd run off to this wilderness to dig for a fortune that simply did not exist. But she had to know more.

"Do you have any family?"

"Not now." He snapped the blade into position. The polished blade glinted menacingly in the lantern light, at odds with the sadness in his voice.

"What does that mean?" She tried not to be nervous.

"It means my brother was recently killed."

"I'm sorry." She read it there on his face, crinkled in the lines fanning the corners of his eyes. Pain. He'd loved his brother. Her heart skipped a beat in sympathy. "Was he your only brother?"

"Yes." Mr. Wyatt Tanner bowed his chin as he bent to turn up the wick, shrugging away her sympathy without regard, as if his loss mattered little.

Yet she suspected the opposite. She began to wonder if Wyatt Tanner wasn't as dangerous and deadly as he was rumored to be.

How her heart ached for him. What would she do if she lost one of her dear sisters? What if she lost Golda? She'd raised her from a baby when their mother had taken ill. She had taught the toddler how to dress herself, as she'd instructed her young sisters in the alphabet and arithmetic. She had protected Golda since the girl had been born, and now what had become of her?

She struggled not to think of Golda's fate. And mightily wished there was something she could do to protect Wyatt from the pain she saw so stark on his rugged face. "Then if you have no other family, you aren't one of those men who's left a wife and children behind so he can dig for gold."

A muscle jumped along the length of his square jaw. "No, I haven't."

My, but his voice was cold. Garnet wondered at that. Apparently he was a little touchy on the subject of a wife and family. Maybe he was the type to never marry. Well, it was certainly better for him to know that of himself, that he wouldn't stay and take responsibility for a family, than for him to run off and leave them to fend for themselves, the way her pa had.

In that, Wyatt Tanner was a better man.

"I'm divorced," he said as he knelt down at her feet.

"Divorced?" Her hand flew to her throat. She was alone with a *divorced* man? In his cabin? *On his bed?*

"She left me, and not the other way around. Couldn't stand me, I guess."

Garnet didn't know what to say. She empathized with the woman. She'd witnessed a lot of marriages, since she had many married friends back home in Willow Hollow, and it was her personal opinion that if divorce ever became more popular, more women would toss out their errant husbands in a flash.

"Garnet, I'll make you a deal."

"A deal?" Her head was spinning. "I don't negotiate with men like you."

He grimaced. "No, your type never does. Haughty, decent women are above men like me."

"Hey, I'm not haughty."

"Haughty. Admit it, Garnet, you are also a tad bit judgmental."

"I wasn't judging—"

"You were," he interrupted, waving that knife in his hand. "Don't forget I saved your life."

"Why, you accidentally shot me in the first place."

"Is that what you think?" Wyatt's laughter boomed in the tiny cabin.

Really, she saw nothing funny about this at all. "I can understand why you'd want to blame your bad shooting on someone else."

"I didn't hit you," he chuckled. "I'm an accurate shot, Garnet."

"But I saw you shoot—"

"The man following you. His rifle fired before I could stop him." Lantern light washed over Wyatt's face, gentle as a touch, illuminating the honesty in his eyes. An honesty as solid as the earth at her feet.

"Then I owe you more gratitude."

"I would rather have whiskey." He winked. "Time to lift your skirts."

"*Excuse me?*"

"I need to bandage your thigh."

Wyatt had never seen a blushing woman. A soft pink shade

crept up from the confining collar at her throat and swept over her oval face. When her mouth wasn't pressed into a straight disapproving line, she was a pretty woman. Her dark hair glistened in the lantern light, framing her delicate features like a great shimmering cloud.

"Ordinarily I wouldn't lift my skirts for a man." She looked hard at her ruffled hem as if she could find some answer to her moral dilemma embroidered there. "I suppose it would never be a proper thing to do, even under these circumstances. But I don't feel well enough to tend the wound myself."

He could see her hand shake; she was weak from blood loss and pain. She'd probably never laid eyes on a bullet wound. "Look, there's no dilemma here. I doubt you want to see the open hole in your thigh, it's pretty bloody. But if you do, I'll step aside—"

"No!" Her quick answer surprised him. She raised one hand as if to keep him from escaping. "I mean, since you did such a fine job before, maybe you could do it again?"

"I'll give you my word. I'll try to control my manly appetites." Wyatt winked at her as he grabbed hold of the ruffled hem and heaved it up over her legs.

He saw her knobby knees piercing through the dust-smudged muslin of her pantaloons. He shook his head. The woman didn't need to be so guarded about her virtue. She could be assured he didn't like bony, sharp-voiced women.

But she blushed, truly embarrassed. He would never understand the propriety some ladies clung to while others had to sell their bodies simply to survive. He'd seen too many injustices in his line of work. A deputy marshal saw all walks of life, all types of people, and everything a man or woman had to do just to survive.

"Hand me that whiskey bottle." He inserted the newly sharpened knife beneath the blood-soaked bandages.

She gasped over the sound of the muslin tearing. Her eyes were wide with pain. Her face turned ashen. Hell, he didn't want her toppling over.

"Hand me the bottle right there, on the edge of the table."

She didn't reach for it, so he said it again. "Hand me the whiskey." Then she quirked a thin arched brow at him, and he lost his temper. "What's your problem? Hand me the damn whiskey."

"No."

"Why the hell not?"

"I don't approve of spirits." The way she raised her lip in disapproval riled him up like an injured bear.

Who knew he'd taken one of those kinds of women into his cabin? She probably wanted the vote, too. "Lady, I know the likes of you is simply too good for my rotgut whiskey, so fine, don't drink it. But I gotta wash this wound out with something. I could use creek water. I got a bucket over in the corner."

"Creek water?" She didn't move at first, but then she turned her stiff chin just enough to spot the flask of whiskey in the center of the table. "You mean, water from Stinking Creek?"

"That's the one."

Her hand trembled as she reached for the bottle. The bright yellow light of the lantern revealed the stiff way her fingers grabbed the glass, as if she were too afraid, or too injured, to do much else.

"I'll allow the whiskey," she whispered, handing him the flask.

Wyatt growled. "I figured you would."

Women. Thank God he didn't have one of them for himself. He lived in the middle of nowhere for a reason. He was far enough away from civilization that no such woman would dream of showing up. And what happened?

One showed up.

With a steady hand he leaned forward just enough to wash the blood from the wound. Whiskey slithered down into the open gash on the woman's thigh.

Garnet gasped, surprised at the sting of the alcohol. She could detect that familiar scent of cheap whiskey Pa often smelled of the rare times he was home. Her gaze slipped to the corner of the cramped cabin where a lump laid beneath a gray wool blanket. Her father. He was alive. She would concentrate on that.

But soon enough her gaze returned to Mr. Tanner. Garnet studied the man's strong features. He was so close she could smell the cigar-and-whiskey scent of him, close enough to see the concern softening the hard-cut features of his face. Of his handsome face. She only now noticed his good looks as he wrapped a fresh strip of muslin around her thigh. Such gentle, careful hands. Feather-light and wonderful.

And there lay the danger. Wyatt Tanner was a miner, dressed from his broad-rimmed hat to the hem of his Levi's in typical prospector's garb. He wasn't a decent sort of man for a woman to start thinking romantic thoughts about. He was a wanderer and a gambler. He was exactly like her father.

Good thing the stage left tomorrow morning. With the way her blood warmed in his presence, Garnet was truly afraid. She'd heard of women falling instantly in love with a man, and she knew it started like this, with an appreciation of his physical attributes.

She knew because it had happened to her mother.

They say love is blind. Well, Garnet Jones would not be blinded by a man's obvious charm and good looks. Or his kindness as he lowered her skirt, her wound now clean and bandaged. Or his smile that lit up the darkness in his eyes and made her heart flip over.

She would be on tomorrow's stage. No matter what.

* * *

Wyatt cursed to himself as he paced around the entire circumference of the little cabin, kicking up dust with each harsh-footed step. He drained the whiskey flask in two long pulls. Fire ignited in his belly, sweet and warm and reassuring. The liquor chased away a deeper emotion he didn't want to feel. Desire. He had looked too darn long at a certain woman's thigh.

Desire was a bad thing. He kept pacing, but not even the cool night air could chase away the memory of her lily-white skin, or the satiny feel of her inner thigh as he'd bandaged her wound. An unmistakable, unbidden tightness gripped his groin. Garnet's soft thigh made him remember what it was like to be with a woman.

The last woman he had made love to was his wife, the woman who taught him he could never be good enough. She'd left him for someone who was. A banker's son who was home every evening, who didn't travel, who made enough money to keep her in the latest fashions.

Wyatt rubbed his eyes, but the pain didn't relent. Yes, he needed more whiskey. He tossed down the bottle before he realized his liquor supply was in the cabin. Where she was with her petal-soft thighs and woman's curves. She smelled like roses. Sweet, wild, gentle.

Just his damn luck.

Wyatt sat down at the creek's bank and stared into the small glimmer of water that slowly lapped over large stones. The quiet motion of water blended with the other night sounds. Listening, Wyatt was content that the world was still the same, even if his cabin had been invaded by a highly proper woman, truly his worst nightmare.

If only he could forget how she felt in his arms. Her long dark hair had cascaded like water over his shoulder, absorbing all the colors of night. Her slender, fine-boned hand had rested on his forearm, so small when compared to his own big-boned strength.

This desire for her was enough to scare him. But then she had done something worse. She had said thank you. Those two words clawed at his chest like trapped mice trying to escape.

The last thing he wanted was the woman's thanks. It wasn't that he was unaffected by her appreciation. He was afraid of it. All the years with his family, then on his own since he was fourteen, then as a lawman, his suspicious nature had kept him alive. Trust no one. It was a good—and safe—motto to live by.

But it made him an awfully lonely man.

And Garnet Jones had to burst into his life with her beautiful dark hair and fine-featured face and lily-soft thighs, and remind him exactly how lonely he was.

Wyatt cupped some of the creek water in the palm of his hand. He doused his forehead, hoping to wash away some of the unrelenting pain that drummed through his head and ached in his heart.

But it didn't. He feared nothing could.

* * *

A muffled bang jarred Garnet from the depth of a murky sleep. She felt as if she were drowning, submerged in a deep lake of water. It was as if she could see the light at the surface of the lake, but she had to struggle for it. She fought, incapable of pulling herself awake. She felt unable to breathe . . . and then suddenly she burst into the morning, already drained.

She blinked. A door stood wide open, letting in the gentle peach light of early morning.

Wyatt's dark gaze met hers. He stood as imposing as the wilderness outside, his long legs spread and his feet braced solidly on the floor. She stared at him, blinking. Her head hurt terribly, her whole body ached. She was so thirsty, the inside of her mouth was dry as sand and her tongue felt swollen.

Then he spoke. "I've been shot before. Nothing feels worse. At least nothing you live through. Here, I brought you some water."

Garnet opened her mouth, but she could find no words. No one had ever waited on her before. In her entire life, she'd been the one taking care of others. No one worried over her. No one was concerned if she was tired or hungry or thirsty or hurt. But this handsome miner did.

"Your hand isn't steady. Let me hold it for you." He knelt at her side and lifted the tin cup to her mouth.

"No, I'm perfectly capable—" Water rushed over her bottom lip. Cool, refreshing. She squeezed her eyes shut, cutting off the sight of the concern in his gaze. He still had a strange hold on her, as if her body had decided to thrum with life no matter what she wanted. She struggled to quiet the rapid beat of her heart and the thud of blood in her ears.

"Is that enough?"

She nodded. His nearness made her dizzy. She pulled herself up into a sitting position, and the full force of her condition hit her with the weight of a falling anvil. Her leg burned with pain, and she almost cried out loud.

"Careful." He caught her hand with both his larger ones. "You haven't gone and developed a fever on me, have you?"

"No." Of that, she was certain. And fortunate. Weakness washed through her like an illness, and it shamed her. To be dependent on a man now, on this man who made her body tingle in ways she knew spelled troubled. Why, she had to get up, had to help Pa, had to leave this cabin and Wyatt Tanner behind.

Well, there was only one solution, and it involved putting her feet on the floor and standing, then walking, then running, no matter how awful she felt. She pushed back the covers. "Excuse me."

"Where do you think you're going?"

"Home. Just like you wanted." And she wanted it, too. She missed Willow Hollow with its clean, tree-lined streets and neat shops. And her own bed in the western corner of the house, too hot in the summer, but hers all the same.

"You aren't moving until I say you are." He used his greater strength to push her back in bed. The humor in his voice was warm and as intimate as a shared secret. It lured her as mightily as his touch. "You just rest, Garnet. Let me fix you breakfast. Then we'll see."

"But—"

"No arguments. Remember, I'm considered a dangerous man in these parts. You'd better do as I say." He might be teasing her, but there was no denying his power. He towered over her, strong and vital, by far the most dangerous male she had ever encountered in her life.

Helpless against him, Garnet sank onto the mattress and melted into the pillows.

He smiled. "Besides, I doubt your father will wake up before full daylight." Then he strode away, leaving her without the ability to speak, his boots thudding dully on the packed earth floor.

"Has he gained consciousness yet?"

"On and off." He knelt before the potbellied stove along the back wall of the tiny cabin and pulled open the squeaky door. "He should be well enough to manage a trip, as long as you're there to take care of him."

"What about my sister?"

Wyatt struck a match, hesitating for just a moment before he lit the kindling. Fire crackled to life, and he added a small stick of dried wood. "I tried tracking her early this morning."

"Oh." Worry trembled in her voice, soft as morning as inviting as a lark's song. "Do you think—"

"Anything could have happened. Could be bad news but your sister may have found her way to town and could be enjoying breakfast as we speak." He added more wood to the fire. "There are a lot of lonely men in these parts who would be more than happy to make sure a lost woman got everything he could give her. Not me, of course. But some men."

"I see."

Wyatt winced. He'd sounded almost as desperate as the men he scorned, pining after their wives and mothers and hometowns, for the comfort a woman's touch brought to their lives. And the beauty.

Well, he'd never known that side of things. Always figured it had never existed. So, before he said anything even more foolish, Wyatt clamped his jaw shut and went about his usual chores. But there was nothing usual about this morning.

He could feel the weight of her gaze on his back a he stirred up the pancake batter. He could hear her unspoken questions heavy in the thick air between them Yet silence reigned as the open door allowed fresh air into the cabin and the sun threw light over the dim corners, chasing out the shadows and the memory of last night.

He glanced over his shoulder. Yes, she was watching him. Her wide eyes catalogued his every movement, examining him as if she could see the quality of his character in the way he stirred the pancake batter or greased the frying pan.

She was different than he had imagined last night in the dark. She was tall, but willowy. She appeared too thin, as if she often ate much less than she should or worked far too hard. It was in the prim set of her mouth and the unadorned gray dress she wore. Only her hair appeared the same as he remembered, cascading as it did down her back, tousled and wild and free.

He sighed heavily, unsure what to do. He didn't want to live ten miles from a woman, much less share a cabin with one, even for a morning. And any fool could see she was in obvious pain. What if she were unable to travel? Would she have to stay here with him until her wound healed?

The coffee was done boiling, so he tugged a tin cup from the shelf, wiped it out with the tail of his shirt, and poured coffee into it. The bitter black liquid steamed, and he gripped the handle carefully.

She shrank as he stepped nearer, her blue-green eyes widening. Wyatt set the cup on the shelf by the bed, leaning close enough to her that he could smell the scent of her body and feel the heat of her skin.

"I'll give you the cup first," he said quietly, stepping backward away from the brush of her hair that had nearly touched his hand. "I only have one."

She didn't blink as she gazed up at him. "Thank you, Wyatt."

She looked different in the light of day. Softer. Smaller. More womanly. Last night she had only been a form in the night. Now she was a supple woman, thin but shapely. He noticed her gentle curves, from her bosom all the way down to her ankles.

"Breakfast will be along shortly." He turned his back on her, remembering his duties at the stove. "It's time to wake your father and see if he'll take breakfast."

"I'll help you." She offered too quickly, as if she were uncomfortable with him, too. "It should be my job to take care of Pa from now on. He is my father and my responsibility."

"Yes." And he was glad of it. Eugene was a difficult patient, and Wyatt couldn't shake the feeling that the old man couldn't be trusted. "Is there anything else I can get you before I put the pancakes on to fry?"

Her lush mouth pursed into a rigid line. Her gaze dropped to the floor. "I need to use the, ah, privy."

She said the last word as if it were something to be ashamed of. He grabbed a bucket out from beneath the table. He dropped it at her feet. "Here, use this. I'll empty it for you."

"No." Her spine stiffened, and her chin flew up. "I mean, I can't let you—I mean, I'd rather visit the privy myself."

"Then stand up." He offered her his outstretched hands. He watched as she gazed up at his face, measuring, and hesitated, then wrapped her slim long fingers around his. He felt the bunch of her arm muscles as she pulled herself upward, and he pulled, too, helping her to her feet.

But just as her feet found the floor, her injured leg buckled and she lost her balance. Unable to stop, she tumbled forward into his chest. He heard her "oof!" when she hit him full-length, and her small body pressed intimately against his.

His arms caught her and held her close, and he didn't know why, but he couldn't let go. He could feel the pillows of her breasts against his chest and the softness of her belly against his groin. A gentle warmth spread through him, a pleasing sensation that reminded him of a cheerful fire on a cold night, the way home felt after a long journey.

"My leg will be just fine," she said, all blushing determination as she pushed off his chest to stand on her own. Pure steel she was, a true spitfire beneath that prim and proper schoolmarm appearance.

"Here." He offered her his arm. "Lean on me. I'll help you outside."

Garnet stiffened, already experienced in what it was like to touch that rock-hard man. Her blood tingled just thinking of it. "No. I can walk. I *will* walk."

It was the tone of her voice that irritated him. Independent. Stubborn. Wyatt's pride stung at the sound of it. "Fine."

He would do better to remember she didn't need him. Or want him. Women were picky in their choice of men—and it all boiled down to how much money he made. And if that truth hurt, well, he'd survived bigger wounds. She clearly didn't want his help, even though she looked ready to faint at any moment.

With amazing fortitude, she hobbled toward the threshold and the serene stillness of the morning. Lark and sparrow trilled merrily. A breeze rustled the alders in the yard and the soft folds of her skirt, so that the fabric hugged her body, hinting at the curve of her hip and fanny. Despite the beautiful autumn morning, the air crisp with the threat of frost, Wyatt couldn't seem to look at anything but her.

"Garnet, is that you?" A rusty-sounding voice shattered the peace.

"Pa!" Garnet whirled around, her affection for the old man shining in her eyes. Her own pain didn't stop her as she made fast progress across the cabin.

She doesn't look at me like that, Wyatt observed. Warm, happy, animated. He turned to his stove and saw the damn contraption needed more fuel. He was more than happy to bolt from the room, leaving father and daughter to their reunion.

CHAPTER FOUR

Garnet sank to her knees beside the pallet in the corner. Pain shot through her thigh, but she felt only relief at the sight of the man before her, looking so weak, so frail. "Pa."

"I knew I could count on you, girl." His voice was rough like gravel and as familiar as her dreams. His eyes smiled hello, but there were darker shadows within, secrets and perhaps worse.

Oh, would she always be such a silly goose? Always it was like this, the first look at her father had her heart strumming with love like a guitar strung too tight. She knew full well Pa would never be the father she needed, not to the little girl who always ran to greet him when he came home from his wandering, earnestly sitting at his feet after the supper dishes were done to listen to his fabricated tales from this gold rush or that.

Always she pined for a love he said he had for her, but she'd learned the hard way Pa's words and deeds were two different things.

Pa always left her and the family behind, always saying the words they wanted to hear; worse, the words she needed to hear. That he loved her. His family was everything. He would never leave, not this time. Everything was different now. But they were lies—no, worse than lies. Pa's promises had been intentional manipulations to get what he wanted, vows he always planned to break.

Oh, she hadn't wanted to believe such things about her father, but time proved her right every time. He always left in the dark of night, stealing from her savings jar, stealing from poor Ma's reticule, and running away to another adventure that wasn't. To another mining camp where he could drink as he wanted and escape all responsibilities.

She'd accepted a long time ago that her father would never change his ways, no matter what he said.

But now, seeing the gladness as big as the Montana sky right there, shining in his eyes, Garnet still wanted to believe this time would be different. That it was still possible to dream of what might be if Pa would stay home like other fathers and tend the land. The hardship would be less, the poverty more bearable with the jolly old man's laugh. Ma would have lived, would have smiled often and merrily just to see this now-weathered, unshaven face across her kitchen table.

Garnet shook herself from her thoughts. It was simply wasted time to daydream of what might be, and what might have been. It was foolish to wish for such things that could never come true.

"You're looking better than I expected." She reached out to lay her hand along his forehead.

It was cool. She'd never felt so relieved. Clearly the serious fever he had been suffering from when Mr. Tanner had written her had now broken. Pa was on the mend. As long as she could walk on her leg, they could leave on this morning's stage. But first, they had to find Golda. She tried not to worry about all that could have happened to her dear sister. Terrible images filled her mind.

"Garnet?"

"Yes." She looked down into Pa's blue eyes that twinkled with warmth. He truly appeared glad to see her. "Is there something you need? The coffee is done boiling."

"Not coffee." His weathered, knuckle-swollen fingers wrapped around her wrist, binding her to him with surprising strength for an ill man. "Money. Did you bring enough to get us all home?"

"I came all this way through uncivilized territory and lost poor Golda to who knows what fate, and all you can ask about is how much money I have?" Garnet twisted her arm from his grip. She ought to walk away and leave the old man stranded here, or at least give him a good swift thwack in the head. Maybe it would smack some sense into that unused brain of his.

"Garnet, don't be like that. I only ask because I'm concerned we might not be able to make it back home."

"You're a liar." Oh, she could see right through her father's innocent request. She climbed to her feet, gritting her teeth. Pain burned through her injured thigh, and yet it was nothing compared to the hurt done to her heart just now. "All you ever care about is getting your hands on money without having to work for it."

"Mind your mouth, girl. I'm warnin' you!"

"Well, I'll have you know I slaved away in an airless schoolroom teaching ungrateful children how to diagram sentences and perform long division no matter how tired I was, or bored, or sick to death of being called horse-face by the big boys in the back of the class when they thought I couldn't hear them. And then I came home and took care of my sisters and worked the farm long into the night and all through the summers—"

"That's enough." Pa held up one hand, half-sitting up, surprisingly strong for one who had only just narrowly escaped death by brain fever. "You misunderstand me, Garnet. I know your pain. I hurt for your struggles. This time I—"

"You're not getting my money, you . . . you thief." She steeled her heart. If her father truly cared about her, he would never have left home, never broken Ma's heart, never left Garnet to take far too much responsibility for a girl so young. The years had not been easy.

Fortunately, she knew just who to blame. "I came here to fetch you because it was my duty and because I didn't want you stealing some poor man's money who was kind enough to take you in and care for you in your illness. And look how you repay me. Ooh!"

Red blazed behind her eyes, and she wanted to yell really loud and do something with her hands. Something that would involve breaking hard objects. But a sensible woman didn't turn to violence and didn't lose her temper. No matter how great the temptation.

Well, her heart was just hurting, as it always did. That old deep ache from her childhood, from a little girl wanting her father's love. Like a scar, it was always there, darn it, and she knew full well Pa would never be any different. He would never love her. So why did it hurt so much? Feelings made no sense, and such conflicts only ended with tears and grief and pain.

Garnet turned her back on the man who'd fathered her, determined to do her duty as she always did. It wasn't because she loved the old lazy liar. She just needed to know she'd done all she could to be the best daughter and best person in her power.

Trying to tamp down her anger, she reached for the same cloth Wyatt had used to open the stove door, intending to check on the fire, when the sound of a gunshot shattered the peace of the still morning. She gasped, one hand flying to her throat. Wyatt!

Fear launched her toward the threshold as a man's confident voice rang from outside. She only knew that the voice did not belong to Wyatt.

"Tanner! I got myself a loaded rifle."

"Lowell, put that thing away before you hurt yourself." That was Wyatt's voice, low and powerful and as mysterious as the darkest night.

Whatever the trouble, Garnet knew Wyatt could protect her from it. She thought of the dangerous man who'd followed her from town last night. Could he have returned to harm her again?

"If you don't hand over that woman in your cabin, then I'll have to shoot you dead."

She eased around the doorway, squinting against the bright rays of the morning sun. There was Wyatt, pressed up against the stable wall with a cocked gun in his hand. His black gaze met hers and held.

"I'm not holding Garnet hostage." Wyatt nodded once in her direction. "She's free to go."

"I don't believe you." The young man gestured with his rifle, ready to shoot. "Throw down your gun, Tanner. I'm here to free the woman."

Watching Wyatt, jaw tensed and muscles hard, his body ready to fight, Garnet knew his reputation as a dangerous man in this lawless wilderness was well earned. He looked able to take on an entire army—and win. With care, he tossed his revolver, and the small handgun landed in the dust directly outside the door, glinting in the peaceful morning sunshine.

"That's more like it, Tanner."

Wyatt drew a second revolver, carefully so the gunman couldn't see, and Garnet couldn't stop her smile. Her valiant rescuer wasn't the brightest of men.

Then a young woman ran out of the brushes, arms outstretched. A plump, rosy-faced girl dressed all in the palest pink. "Garnet! Garnet, is that you?"

"*Golda*? " She couldn't believe her eyes.

"I was so afraid when I saw you kidnapped by that . . . that ruffian." Young Golda dashed through the streaks of morning sunshine and into Garnet's arms. "I'm so thankful you're alive, that we got here in time. I spent all night fearing the very worst."

"I am fine. But where were you?"

Golda blushed, stepping back. "I was in the forest."

"All night?" Garnet noticed her sister's torn and dirt-streaked pink dress, yet with the smile bright on her face she didn't look worse for the wear. "You spent the entire night alone? You must have been frightened."

She blushed. "Not exactly."

Garnet's gaze flew to the young man and his rifle. "You spent the night with him? Did he try to harm you? Golda, you must tell me the truth."

"Lance didn't insult me, if that's what you mean." Her blue eyes twinkled merrily. "He rescued me from the wolves early this morning. I climbed a tree to escape them, you know, and he was out hunting for breakfast and came upon me. He took me home, fed me a wonderful breakfast, and even offered to rescue you. How's Pa? Is he still alive?"

"For now. We can talk about that in a moment." Garnet looked over her sister's head and caught sight of Wyatt's tall, broad-shouldered form. Such an impressive man, so strong and capable. He made that boyish-looking miner appear a weakling in comparison.

So, that was Lance? That unkempt miner? Brown-blond hair peeked out from beneath a dirty, misshapen hat. Well, he wasn't so impressive at all. Golda surely could not be smitten with him. A man like that was trouble of the worst kind. Any sensible woman would recognize that right off.

* * *

Wyatt was unhappy with the arrangement. Now two women crowded his small cabin, claiming it as if it were their own. He had been obliged to haul wood and water while Garnet and Golda had fed their pa, marveling over how very well he was, considering he'd been deathly ill with brain fever only a few months ago.

Wyatt stood in the doorway to his cabin and stared at the chaos. Water boiled on the stove. A washtub Lance had hauled from somewhere in town sat directly in the middle of the one tiny room. Eugene lay on his back, a small grin on his chubby, wizened face, faking weakness simply to get out of the work.

Garnet and Golda were finishing up the dishes. His breakfast dishes. The breakfast he had made for himself and hadn't been afforded the opportunity to eat because of this damned intrusion. He stood in the door, scowling, a dark anger building in his chest. But neither of the women glanced up from their work to notice. Garnet, her dark lustrous hair tied back with a small length of muslin, stood at his wobbly table, her arms plunged into one of his only two buckets, sudsing his dishes.

His dishes! What would they do next? Wash his clothes? His entire cabin?

Garnet looked up from her work, turning her soft face toward him for the first time since her sister arrived. She looked appealing with the sparkle of happiness in her eyes. She was still too pale, but a small grin warmed the stern lines on her face and she looked young and beautiful.

"I left some flapjacks for you," she said. "Here, this dish and cup are clean. Golda just needs to dry them for you."

She gestured toward her young sister. The girl with the golden curls nervously wiped his tin cup. The cup he'd had for years, that had been banged and dented and even kicked by his horse. The cup he had never remembered washing. Not once. Ever.

Wyatt shook his head. "Where did you get the soap?"

"Young Mr. Lowell," Garnet answered brightly, as if the man had brought something more precious than gold. "He's turned out to be quite handy for a worthless, ne'er-do-well prospector."

"Garnet!" Golda scolded, setting the newly dried tin cup down on the table with a thunk. "Please, do not speak of Lance that way. He practically saved my life and risked his to rescue you."

"I didn't need rescuing and besides, it isn't proper to call a man by his given name." The softness of Garnet's mouth retreated into a severe frown. "Really, Golda, one would think you had no brain at all in that head of yours. Lance is just like Pa, can't you see that? And Pa's been nothing but an aimless dreamer. Look how he's treated us all our lives."

Golda's pink mouth pinched into an obvious pout, although she said nothing.

Wyatt felt a distaste burn like acid in his belly. This pouting display was another thing he so greatly disliked about women. He dared to walk past the two females, careful to keep his distance, on the way to the cook-stove. The coffeepot, apparently not yet a victim to Garnet's dishwater, sat neatly on the blackened stove top. If there was a God in the heavens, then the coffee would be burned, boiling hot, and thick as mud. Which, of course, was the next best thing to a full flask of whiskey.

He turned to face the women and held out his hand. "Give me the cup."

Golda jumped as if he had drawn his revolver and shot her through the heart. Her small plump hand flew to her chest and stayed there as if to stop the imaginary flow of blood. Some women, Wyatt shook his head, they were so jumpy.

"My cup?"

Garnet scowled, adding an impoverished look to her already stern face. She reached with her soapy hands across the rinse water and grabbed the newly cleaned tin. She held it out to him, clearly unable to step forward and bridge the short distance between them. She might be standing, but Wyatt could see the strain carving deep lines across her forehead and the pain pinching the corners of her eyes. Her leg had to be hurting her. Yet she wasn't saying a word.

He had to respect her. She was tough and uncomplaining and loyal. And yet there was a softness in her, too. A truly rare female. Wyatt had known little comfort in his life and even less love, not as a boy in a rough, chaotic household and not as a lawman working in the lawless West. He'd seen enough that he admired anyone with true strength. He admired Garnet.

He stepped forward and took the cup from her wet fingers. Small soap bubbles clung to the sparkling clean rim. "Thanks."

There was a frankness in her eyes, in those blue-and-green specked depths, and a kindness in her soul that he could not dismiss.

"I washed the coffeepot and then boiled fresh for you." She turned, plunging her hands inside the soapy bucket and coming up with his only fork.

"You washed my coffeepot?"

"Disgusting coffee stains and the most deplorable-looking mung were caked on the bottom of the poor pot. You have no notion how hard I had to scrub to get it off. Really, Wyatt, you should wash your possessions more often. It's unhealthy."

He tried to ignore her civilizing advice. Great. Just great. Now his treasured cup of morning coffee would taste of that strong lye soap she was using.

Wyatt reached for the stained, torn shirt he used as a hot pad and grabbed the pot from the stove. He filled the clean cup and watched with disappointment as the coffee poured out thin, brown, and watery. Where was the bitter blackness? The thick rich brew that looked like mud?

Wyatt fought to keep a lid on his temper. Since a man couldn't survive on this weak brew, he grabbed the closest whiskey bottle from the shelf, one of a dozen, and snapped open the seal. He poured a liberal dollop of liquor into his cup before retightening the cap. When he turned, he saw both women staring at him in disapproval.

"This is my shack," he reminded them.

Garnet clucked her tongue like a seasoned schoolmarm. "I did not say a word."

"That look you're giving me sure does."

Hell, he hadn't rescued the damn woman from the wolves just to have her take over his life, wash his cup, make his coffee.

Grumbling, Wyatt rescued his plate of pancakes from the oven, grabbed his only fork from Golda's trembling fingers and, armed with his whiskey-laden cup of coffee, marched outside.

He would eat by the creek where only nature and no women were there to bother him.

* * *

"He looks vicious," Golda whispered the instant Wyatt had disappeared from sight. "Those eyes of his. Did you notice how black and soulless they are? I bet he's a wanted man hiding out from the law in this godforsaken wilderness. He's killed somebody. Maybe even a lot of somebodies. Everyone in town said he was dangerous."

Garnet frowned at her sister's bothersome imagination. "Really, be realistic. Mr. Tanner may be highly disagreeable, but he did save my life and Pa's. He carried me here, even though it was a long way, and tended my wound. He even gave me the cabin for the night."

"Well, I just don't like him," Golda wailed nervously. She dropped the frying pan and bent to retrieve it. "He terrifies me."

"Well, he should," she snapped, her nerves suddenly on edge.

Had Golda always been this way? Garnet wrung out a rag she'd torn from that old shirt in the corner and began wiping down the table with swift, vigorous strokes. Her rag came up muddy, so she rinsed and scrubbed a second time. "Wyatt Tanner is a dangerous, unpredictable man and any sensible woman ought to be terrified of him. But he took care of me and I am grateful."

"You're not making any sense."

"I'm making perfect sense. Go throw out this water and bring in fresh. We've got a lot more washing to do."

"Garnet, tell me you don't mean you have feelings for that horrible ruffian. You spent the night with him."

"I was here with Pa, and Wyatt remained outside the entire night." Garnet felt heat creep across her face. She bowed her chin and scrubbed the table as hard as she could, determined to wipe away every last speck of dirt and stain.

But truly, she just didn't want Golda to see the truth in her eyes. Old maid Garnet Jones had feelings. Had wants and needs and dreams. And those dreams were no one's business. Especially not her little sister's.

"Go on now," she ordered, more gruffly than she meant. "We've got more washing to do. Fetch some water."

Golda's eyes grew round. "I'm not going outside. *He's* out there. Oh, I wish Lance—ah, Mr. Lowell— were here. I'd feel safer knowing he could protect me in case that outlaw becomes violent."

"Stop the theatrics." Garnet shook her head. Of all her sisters, Golda had always been the most senseless: a dreamer, resembling their pa more than anyone wanted to admit. "Fine, then you can strip the sheets and blankets from both the bed and Pa's pallet, and I'll go outside and fetch the water."

"Thanks, Garnet." True appreciation shone in Golda's eyes. "I am probably being a silly goose, but I can't tell you what it was like for me to have spent the night alone in the wilderness. I'm still frightened."

Garnet's heart pinched. Her youngest sister was only fifteen, and a sheltered fifteen at that. "Yes, I understand. Now get to work. I will return shortly."

She limped to the door, where daylight slanted through the threshold. How good the sunshine felt. A persistent cool breeze fanned across her face and ruffled her skirts. She moved gingerly down the steps, now that she was out of her sister's sight . . . out of anyone's sight. She didn't need to act as strong. Nobody was around to see how weak she was, how much she hurt.

She scanned the small dirt yard and saw no sign of Mr. Tanner. As she limped slowly, searching for him, she mulled over her problem. Mr. Lance Lowell had been left alone with Golda in his tent for an extended time this morning. Garnet seriously doubted any improprieties had occurred, but she had spotted the adoring look in her sister's eyes every time she looked at the young miner. Was Golda in love? She couldn't be, could she?

This morning, when Mr. Tanner had finished cussing out Lance Lowell for foolishly threatening him and for carelessly brandishing a deadly weapon, Wyatt had stalked angrily off, swearing they had all better be gone by the time he returned from the privy. Golda had been terrified, but Garnet suspected Mr. Tanner had a good temperament beneath all the irritability. Despite all the trouble they caused him, he'd been nothing but thoughtful and helpful.

Well, the three of them would leave today, directly after breakfast. As long as there was no complication with her sister and the handsome young miner. Fortunately, Mr. Lance Lowell had offered to try to borrow a horse and a cart so as to haul their old sick pa to town. She hoped he would be strong enough to climb aboard the stage.

They had discussed plans over the tasty pancakes. Garnet had sat next to her sister while Mr. Lance Lowell had perched across the table, his lusty eyes glued to young Golda. He confirmed Garnet's suspicions. He was nothing but trouble.

Her stomach even now clenched at the thought. She could see what he wanted. She knew the minds of men. Hadn't she watched their pa wander through life, even more useless than most, like a little boy aching after his pleasures?

Even now, as an old man, sick because of his wandering, he would never realize the responsibilities he had left behind. A mortgage. Land to farm. A woman who loved and needed him, who had believed in him and died without him. Children to feed and clothe. Crops to bring in and interest payments to make. Responsibilities Garnet had shouldered since she was old enough to understand them.

She would not—would not—allow Golda to become entrapped by the same fate their mother had. Bound by poverty, pining after a man who was too immature to love anyone but himself, it could only end in heartbreak. As long as Garnet lived she would not allow Golda to have such a life of broken dreams.

How fortunate the stage was leaving this very day. And how unfortunate poor love-struck Lance would have to stay behind.

"Mr. Tanner?"

She found him sitting quietly beside the creek. With one elbow planted on his knee, he gazed off into the distance, at majestic blue mountains close enough to touch. In solitude, Wyatt looked as if he were part of this larger-than-life landscape. An empty plate sat beside him. He hugged the tin cup with one broad hand.

He turned to look at her with those eyes as dark as midnight, and her heart fluttered like leaves in a wind. "How's the coffee?"

"Passable." He shrugged one perfect shoulder. "Except for the strong lye soap taste."

"I hadn't realized." It was just that there had been so much crud crusted to the bottom and she had been so bent on cleaning it thoroughly. It had taken so much soap. Perhaps she hadn't rinsed the coffeepot very thoroughly. "I'm sorry."

He turned away. The creek rushed by inches from his booted feet. "Are you ready to leave?"

"Not yet." Garnet's courage faltered. Like a winged bird, it was ready to take flight and leave her without any bravery at all. "That's what I need to speak to you about."

"What's wrong?" He set the tin cup down beside the plate with a slow, deliberate motion. The way he anchored it between the large pebbles of the creek bank somehow looked dangerous. Garnet couldn't say why until she gazed into his eyes, and gasped.

Concern burned there. Soulless eyes, Golda had called them. Nothing could be further from the truth. They lived with strength, with a vibrant male power that could overwhelm a woman, leave her unable to breathe.

He took one step toward her, his big body moving powerfully, his strong arms swinging with his gait. She remembered the steel strength in those arms. Remembered how he had held her, carried her, tended her wound when she was too shaky to do it herself.

"Nothing is wrong, Wyatt. I just wanted to thank you. You have done so very much for me and my family, and yet we have no way to repay your hospitality."

"You can stop washing my things." He wasn't wearing a hat, and the breeze tousled his black hair, tossing a shank of it over his forehead. How rakish he looked. How handsome. No such man had ever shown her the slightest interest or bit of regard. She liked how he looked at her, and how she felt just being with him.

Of course, she was just being silly. Wyatt Tanner wasn't sweet on her. He was simply being kind to an injured woman. She knew it. It just felt so nice to be treated this way, to be looked at by a man, truly looked at, as if he could see past her flaws and her plain features to the real her deep inside.

"It's a deal, then." She tried to smile. She ought to be happy that they were leaving, that he wanted her out of his cabin and away from his possessions. "I'll refrain from doing any more housework. If you lack the good sense for basic hygiene, then it's not my job to try and enlighten you."

That made him laugh, as she had hoped. Humor lit his dark eyes and eased the lines worn into his face by sun and worry and time. When he laughed, it was easy to see he was a decent man and not dangerous, as rumors made him out to be.

"Thank you for allowing me my ignorance in the ways of cleanliness." He winked.

Charmed, she could not help but tease him. "If you ere to want me to do a little laundry for you, perhaps—"

"Save me from lye-toting, woman," he pleaded. A slow smile pulled up the corners of his mouth. Something amusing burned in his eyes as he stepped close. Too darn close for propriety's sake. . . . Too darn close for her preferences.

Her heart slammed to a stop in her chest. Warm sparkles flickered to life in her veins, and her gaze latched onto his mouth. "I-I need to get back to the cabin. To Pa. We're getting ready to leave."

"And I need to get some work done." Wyatt planted his broad fists on his hips, the movement serving to emphasize the bulk of his arms and shoulders, and the inherent strength in them. So much power. So much protection. "I guess this is good-bye."

"I guess it is." Good-bye. She hated that word more than ever before. She didn't want to leave, as illogical as it was. She certainly could not stay here in a tiny shanty with a man too much like her pa. What could there ever be between them? Even if she sort of, maybe just a little bit, liked Wyatt. Garnet knew she had to catch that stage.

Bugs buzzed by, birds chattered, leaves crinkled in cadence with the hot breeze. Wyatt took one step closer so that they were nose-to-nose. So close that Garnet moved back, and stumbled. His right hand shot out, grasping her about the upper arm, righting her and at the same time holding her captive. Black flecks burned in his obsidian eyes. The blood stalled in her veins. Was he going to kiss her?

But he turned away without a word. She watched his back as he ambled toward the creek. He stood at the shallow bank, a rugged man without anyone to lean on. A man strong enough to stand on his own in this dangerous wilderness, tough enough to survive in this lawless land.

She'd forgotten all about asking him for the water. She'd forgotten about everything but the ache in her chest for love and a dream she could never have.

"Garnet! Where are you?" Golda raced out of the cabin, screaming hysterically. "Come quick. Pa's gone!"

"What do you mean, he's gone?" Garnet hefted the water-filled bucket from the creek. "Where is he?"

"I don't know. He is not in his bed."

"Perhaps he is using the privy."

"I checked. He's nowhere to be found." Golda dashed across the dusty yard and straight into Garnet's arms, already sobbing. "He didn't leave us, right?"

"Why that—that pleasure-seeking sneak!" Garnet fumed. He'd been moaning long and hard about how weak he was back in the cabin when there was work to be done. And just moments ago when he learned they were leaving for the stagecoach.

Why, he must have wanted to stay in this uncivilized territory. So he just ran off. Like always. He'd been too much of a liar to tell her the truth, to spare her this betrayal.

"I should have expected it." Garnet blinked back tears. Anger and hurt mixed in her chest, causing the worst pain.

Golda sniffed. "I can't believe he *left* without even saying good-bye."

"You know this isn't the first time." Garnet held the weeping girl and gently patted her plump back. There was nothing comforting she could say about the man who had sired them. This action was entirely typical. Now she feared for Wyatt's accumulation of gold dust, if he had any. Had Pa stolen it?

"Did you ever see Pa up and about when I was out of the

cabin?" Garnet asked in a gentle voice. No use upsetting the girl further.

"N-not really." Golda stepped away from their embrace to delicately wipe her nose on her sleeve. "I mean, I wasn't sure."

"You weren't sure?"

"I mean, he asked me not to say anything because he really wasn't strong enough to get far. I believed him. He's our father."

"You should have told me." With a heavy heart, Garnet knew she had been fooled—as she always was—by Pa's seeming innocence. When would she learn? When would she ever stop aching for him to love her, just once?

"What are we going to do now?" Golda sniffled.

She would be angry later, after she'd taken care of her sister. "I guess there's naught to be done but make some coffee and look at our options. The stage is still running today. I say we make plans to head east before snow flies. Maybe I can even be home for the start of the school term. All is not lost. Not yet, anyway."

Yes, that was a bracing thought. She hobbled slowly toward the cabin. At least she had done her duty to her father and to herself and could return home with a clear conscience.

Now, where did she put her reticule?

"Garnet?" Golda scratched her head as she studied the contents of Wyatt's rather empty shelves next to the stove. Empty except for the whiskey bottles, that is.

"Do you need help with the coffee grinder?" Garnet asked, wearily. Her injured thigh was paining her something fierce.

In answer, Golda held up the cloth reticules ... the empty reticules. Tears trickled down her cheeks.

"*Oh, no!*" Garnet bolted to her feet. "It can't be. Not again."

Golda only cried harder.

"*Did he take our money?*" It couldn't be true. It just couldn't.

"All of it." Golda dipped her head.

Garnet's knees wobbled. Every last penny? They needed to be on the stage in less than an hour. How were they going to buy their passage home? How could Pa have done this to them?

"I suppose he needed the money," Golda sniffled. "Maybe he needed it real bad."

"We need it worse." Garnet covered her face with her hands. "Don't you see what this means?"

They were stuck in Stinking Creek, Montana.

CHAPTER FIVE

Wyatt returned home from his long day trying to track down the owner of that bloody rifle that had shot Garnet. He'd had no leads, but he'd spent time noticing who seemed short a weapon and who owned a dark horse. He'd been north of town when the stage came and went, and he was sorry about that. He ought to have at least seen Garnet Jones off, bid her farewell.

Hell, he wasn't any good with good-byes. Or relationships. He just wanted to get back to his work, hunting down the murderer who'd robbed him of his brother, and move on. That was all he wanted.

And yet his chest felt hollow. He'd admired Garnet in many ways. He would miss her. He wished her a safe journey home. As he strode down the tree-lined lane, he could almost picture the kind of town she came from— everything in its place, clean streets and well-tended shops and a house with fresh paint, not a speck of dust inside. She'd have all those doodads and gewgaws a woman liked to collect.

And that's as far as he'd let his mind imagine. Soon he'd be wishing he had a woman to call his own, a real home again, possibilities for a family and a future. No, it was best to stick to the hard lessons life had taught him. He was alone in this world, for better or,worse.

* * *

S tuck in Stinking Creek. The truth was unpalatable every time she thought about it. And the more she thought on her problem, the more Garnet could find no solution. They were penniless in a town where the major sources of income came from gambling, prostituting, and prospecting.

Goodness, she wasn't about to gamble . . . not that she had any money to gamble with. And she certainly wasn't going to go knocking on a brothel's door looking for work. That only left prospecting, and by heaven, if she ever met anyone who made a decent amount of money doing that, she'd fall over in a dead faint from surprise.

And that left her good and truly stuck.

"What are we going to do now?" Golda settled down on the only chair in the cabin, careful not to dirty her favorite dimity dress.

"Well, *you're* going to stop sitting around and being so concerned about your looks. Go pack buckets of water from the creek." Garnet heard the anger in her voice, but she couldn't help it. She'd traveled all this way, spending a good portion of her life's savings in passage and coach fare just to be duped out of the rest of it by her own father. "Go on, get up. We've got work to do."

"But, Garnet, I don't want to work."

Had Golda always been this complaining? "You're nearly sixteen years old, and many women your age already have the responsibility of husbands and children."

"Well, I don't. Can't we find someone to loan us the money?"

"Golda! A proper woman doesn't accept money from a decent man, much less from the sort of wanderers who reside in a town like this." Really, Golda was too much like Pa for her own good. "If you want to get back home, you'll get off your fanny."

"But Mr. Tanner would pay to get rid of us, don't you think?"

"I think you've been too pampered for your own good." Garnet clamped her jaw as she hobbled toward the rickety table. "We have to figure out a way to keep food in our bellies and a roof over our heads until the stage leaves next week. *Without* taking advantage of Mr. Tanner."

Golda huffed from the room, and Garnet ached to sit down, but she worried more what Wyatt would say when he came home and found them here. They had no place to go, and there were no decent rooms for rent in all of Stinking Creek, even if they had the money.

It was clear she had to figure out a way to make herself useful, to prove to Wyatt that she could improve his life in exchange for a roof over their heads. She had a week. A week to figure out how to raise enough money to see them home.

Money it had taken her half a lifetime to earn.

* * *

As Wyatt neared his cabin, he heard blessed silence. No women's chatter punctuated the cool air. No scent of lye soap drifted on the evening's crisp breezes. Looked like they were truly gone. Was he sad? He didn't know, but his chest felt tight

He had been a loner for so long, he couldn't remember any other way of life. Even as a small boy growing up in his family, he had been alone. Perhaps it was his father's drinking. Perhaps it was his mother's whining nature. Both parents had only been interested in themselves and satisfying their most pressing needs.

So instead of a family, they were really four people sharing a house. Eating at the table. Sleeping in separate beds at night. Watching Pa drink himself to ruin. Listening to Ma whine and cajole and manipulate her way into having fabric for a new dress, a set of dishes, a fine bay mare when they were too poor to afford food enough for all of them.

No, he had no need of a family or of any other human connection. He'd had his brother. Then fate had intervened.

He kicked open the cabin door and stared into the darkness of the windowless structure. Finally. He might be lonely, but at least he had all the peace and quiet a man could desire.

Then he saw a movement along the shadows of the back wall. An intruder. Was it the same man who'd killed his brother? Before his heart could beat again, he held his cocked revolver in hand.

"Wyatt! No!"

It was a woman's voice. Sweat popped out on the back of his neck. Adrenaline squirted into his blood. His knees shook, and he holstered the gun before his trembling fingers dropped it. Damn, he was glad he hadn't pulled the trigger. What in the blazes was wrong with the woman? He'd nearly shot her.

"Garnet Jones. I thought you had left." His voice boomed through the quiet interior, echoing against the four scrubby walls. "I distinctly remember you promising to leave. Vowing to leave.

Saying good-bye. Packing up your pa."

"Well, yes, we did all those things."

"Then what happened? Explain it to me."

"Well, I meant to catch the stage."

"Meant to? What happened? The horses ran away, an axle broke, the coach was robbed?" He heard a clink of glass and then saw the flare of a match.

She lit the lantern and stood, bathed in its orange glow. "Pa abandoned us."

"You mean he ran off?"

A single nod. Tears stood in her eyes, stubbornly refusing to fall. Despite everything, she did love her father. Why, he couldn't imagine. Eugene had been a weak complainer of a man, jabbering on about his dreams of gold and opulence and a life of wealth and ease. He was a man who hadn't an ounce of gold to his name or a penny in his pockets when he'd fallen ill in the road.

"And that's not all. He stole all our money. Every last penny." A lone muscle jumped in her tightly clenched jaw. "We couldn't leave for home today because we couldn't buy the tickets."

Fire flashed in Wyatt's eyes, dark and dangerous. "I will track him down for you. If he hasn't left the territory, I'll find him."

"You would do that?" She clenched her hands into hard-knuckled fists. "Wyatt, it's far too much trouble. Let him go. I don't want to see that good-for-nothing coward. He's a lily-livered cheat who thinks he can take anything from us just because we're family. He's a damn bastard, that's what he is."

Wyatt leaned against the doorjamb, biting his lower lip so it wouldn't tug into a grin. He'd never seen anything half so funny as prim and proper Garnet Jones cussing like a man.

"I see your smirk," she accused, finger pointing. "Don't you dare find amusement in this. That damn man has betrayed me again, played me for a fool, and you've been drinking entirely too much whiskey if you think this is anything close to being funny. Get your horse. You need to go after him."

"You just said you didn't want your pa back."

"No, but if you think you can track him, then bring me back my money. Do you know how to track? That moonstruck Lance couldn't find any sign in your yard at all, and frankly, I'm not going to be stuck here all winter with a person like you."

"Like me?"

"A worthless miner who can't take responsibilities, that's who." Tears filled her eyes, and it wasn't anger that burned there, but hurt, honest and clear and unmistakable.

Wyatt knew she was speaking about her father, not about him. How deep her heart went, if she could love a man who'd hurt her so much.

"A horrible, worthless miner," she sobbed.

Geez, he had no clue what to do with a crying woman. "Now, I'm not that irresponsible. And I'm no slouch when it comes to tracking, so I can head out right now and see if I can't bring back your money. What your pa hasn't spent, that is. You can count on me, Garnet."

He caught himself reaching out. What did he think he was going to do? Hold her? Comfort her? He didn't have the right. She was pretty and proper, and she didn't want a man like him. No woman did. All she saw was a penniless miner with no valuable property and no assets to satisfy her wants and needs.

Even Garnet, though sensible and tough, felt this way.

Why was he disappointed? He stepped out in the dark, his heart heavy.

"Wyatt?" She called him back. "This is dangerous country. Be careful."

Sincerity shimmered in eyes as deep as a mountain lake, and his heart caught. "Don't worry. I know this land like the back of my hand. I can take care of myself well enough."

With an image of her posed in the threshold, her skirts hugging her slim body, he slipped off into the night, to become part of it. Determination fueled him, and he headed to the stable where his horse waited. Wyatt was intent upon tracking down the lowlife who'd run off on his family and stolen from a woman as hardworking as Garnet.

If Eugene Jones was anywhere in Montana Territory, he was going to pay.

* * *

Garnet tucked the end of the fresh bandage tight and released a long breath. Her thigh hurt like the dickens, but it was healing, thank heavens. She'd developed no fever and the wound itself was not red and festering. Whatever type of man Wyatt Tanner may be, he'd redeemed himself in her eyes yet again.

But her problems remained. There had to be some decent sort of work she could do somewhere in godforsaken Stinking Creek. There had to be a respectable business somewhere. A mercantile or a laundry.

Night was already falling, without signs of Wyatt's return. She thought of the man alone in this wilderness. Remembering his words, she did not doubt his strength or his cunning. A man as rugged and dangerous as Mr. Tanner could certainly hold his own in this uncivilized territory.

Golda stumbled into the cabin, dropping sticks of wood as she went, grumbling.

Weary from scrubbing all day, Garnet climbed to her feet and retrieved the fallen pieces of cedar. The rich fragrance tickled her nose and reminded her of her room at home, of the cedar chest that sat at the foot of her bed and held her treasures—Ma's best sweater, her own knitted dreams of baby afghans and baby clothes that she would probably never have use of. After all, no man had ever wanted to marry her. But the knitted things were nice to hold, nice to think of what-might-have-been if Pa had not been so irresponsible, if Ma had not died.

A bittersweet warmth tugged at Garnet's heart. She missed home so much.

"Garnet, I tore my hem on the stove!" Golda complained.

That must have been the two hundredth complaint today. Garnet took a sustaining breath, uttered a prayer for patience, of which she was running in short supply, and hobbled toward the stove. "We have needle and thread. It's mendable, Golda."

"But it's ruined. It will have to be patched." Golda looked so vulnerable. "Ask Mr. Tanner for some money so we can get out of this awful place."

"I doubt Mr. Tanner has that kind of money to spare." Garnet knelt to stock the fire with dry kindling, then built the cedar in a tent above it. "Fetch me the match tin from the shelf."

Golda moved away to comply, still pouting. Garnet remembered that age well, but had to bite her tongue to keep from upbraiding the girl. They had to work together if they hoped to ever return to Willow Hollow. Wyatt had said that if the snows came, then the stages could not run. What if they were stranded here all winter? The thought was too terrible to contemplate.

Twilight came quickly, draining the last of the light from the room. Garnet thanked Golda for the tin. When she lit the match, the tiny flame chased away some of the darkness. She lit the fire and watched over it to make sure it thrived.

"What was that?" Golda hissed, spinning around to stare at the door.

"I didn't hear anything." The crackle and pop of the kindling was loud. "Maybe it's Wyatt returning home."

"Oh, I hope he found Pa."

"I hope he found my money." Garnet's throat tightened. Her stomach clamped into an unsettled ball. She didn't think of herself as a materialistic woman, but she'd been a schoolteacher for ten long years, and worked hard to stretch every dollar and save every penny. Without it, she wasn't just stuck in Montana Territory. She was broke.

A sharp snapping sound riveted her. "Why, that sounded like the stable door. Wyatt's home."

But another sound, like wood cracking, had her wondering. Wyatt was as quiet as the night, like a ghost who could drift soundlessly. Garnet ordered Golda to keep an eye on the fledgling fire and peered through a crack where the twilight crept between the wallboards.

She didn't see a horse. Wyatt had ridden off on his, so he would have returned with it. A crackle of alarm bolted down her spine. Then a light leaped to life in the stable, a soft orange glow. A lantern's light.

Another warning crackle speared her. Wyatt had left the only lantern behind in the cabin.

That was not Wyatt out there in that stable. In a flash Garnet remembered the out-of-control, dangerous men she'd glimpsed through the windows of the saloons when she'd first arrived in town. Any number of outlaws and killers must inhabit a place like this—with no law, no sheriff, no one to keep the peace.

What if he decided to break into the cabin next? Garnet rushed through the dark, despite her injury, and bolted the door.

"Garnet? What's wrong?" Golda whimpered, spinning from the fire, the yellow light from the meager flames brushing over her, showing her stark fear. "Is it Mr. Tanner? Maybe he's decided to show his true colors. I haven't wanted to tell you, but I do not think he could possibly be a safe or proper protector for a girl like me."

"Hush up and let me think, or there won't be anything left of either one of us for Mr. Tanner to come home to." Garnet wrung her hands.

What if that intruder didn't stop at a barred door? She had no weapon, not that she would use a gun if Wyatt had left her one. She did not approve of violence . . . but then she'd never been alone and afraid in a dangerous place like Montana Territory before.

She may have to amend some of her long-standing, firmly held beliefs.

"Garnet!" Golda stood, the blaze in the stove's belly forgotten. "You didn't tell me what's wrong. I'm a grown woman now. You said so yourself. I can help."

"Hand me a whiskey bottle."

"You can't possibly think to take up drinking at a time like this!" Golda almost wailed.

"Hand it to me." Garnet nodded when Golda obeyed, her face twisted in disapproval of the bottled spirits. "Now, bolt the door after me, and take a bottle for yourself. If anyone threatens you, hit him in the head as he comes through the door."

"You're going to leave me alone?"

"Yes. Quiet, now. Maybe the intruder doesn't know we're here, or he would have sneaked up on us first." Garnet took strength from that thought.

She stumbled out into the black night. No wind rustled the trees, no moon shone above to illuminate the forest. Garnet kept to the shadows, fear growing with every beat of her pounding heart, but anger, too. How dare that man, whoever he was, trespass. How dare he frighten her like this by sneaking around in Wyatt's stable!

By the time she'd reached the nearest corner of the stable, the man inside had doused his lantern. She'd been careful, but maybe he'd heard her approach. Garnet froze and held her breath. No sound came from within, no footstep, nothing.

He had heard her. Oh, maybe this was a harebrained notion, coming out like this. But she wasn't about to sit around in the dark cabin waiting to get attacked. She tightened her hold on the bottle, preparing herself for what was to come.

The quietest footstep whispered against the earth. The leather hinges on the door whooshed open, just the tiniest sound. The hair on the back of Garnet's neck rose. She lifted the bottle over her head, ready to strike, pulse pounding.

Another footfall, then she could see the dark shadow of a man, not as tall as Wyatt, and his shoulders not half so broad, yet broader than poor moonstruck Lance. Then she saw the man's hand and the gun it held. Anger flared and she swung with all her might.

The bottle connected with the side of his head. Glass shattered, and the man cried out, then crumpled to the ground in silence. His gun tumbled out of his slack fingers and kicked up a small puff of dust.

"Oh, Lord! I've killed him." Garnet raced to the man's side. He appeared motionless. His hat rolled off his head. Too bad he'd collapsed in the shadows, because she couldn't see anything of his face, but she could smell both the pungent whiskey and the coppery scent of fresh blood. He didn't appear to be breathing. He didn't seem alive.

Now what did she do? Garnet knelt at his shoulder and extended her hand. She felt the front of his chest and inched her way across to the male-hot skin of his throat. She couldn't find a pulse, but then her hand was shaking too hard to feel anything. Maybe a light would help. She rose, but could not find the man's lantern.

"Golda." She ran for the cabin. "Grab the lantern for me. I think I killed a man."

"Garnet! How could you?" The door swung open to reveal Golda's shadowed face. "You looked before you hit him, right?"

"I'm no fool. It wasn't anyone I knew." Garnet's hand shook as she reached for the tin. The matches inside rattled and she had trouble grabbing hold of one. "I feel sick. I hit him extremely hard. Maybe a little too hard. I'm very strong from working the farm, you know. Even now with Ruby's husband to help."

Garnet thought of her sister, who had married despite all warnings, and her chest constricted. How she wished she were home, safe in her comfortable house, in her kitchen getting a meal ready. Her sisters would be there, talking as they peeled potatoes and set the table.

Golda's hands trembled, too, as she produced the small battered lantern. "Are you afraid to go back outside?"

"Yes. I was hoping you could come with me. All you would

have to do is stand behind me and hold the light. Could you do that?"

"What are you going to do with the body?" Golda's eyes grew round.

"I have no idea." Garnet stumbled down the steps, limping across the uneven earth toward the rear of the cabin. Shadows covered the ground where the forest was thick. The lantern light flickered along the dusty earth.

Garnet stopped at the corner of the stable, but the orange glow revealed no body, no man dead or unconscious. "He was here. Look at the stain. It's blood."

"Oh, no." Golda's head snapped toward the forest. "He's escaped. Maybe he's watching us. Maybe he's waiting for us. Maybe you've made him really mad, Garnet."

"Maybe I did." She knelt to study the drops in the dirt, a steady dribble that could only mean a serious cut. Well, at least she had stopped him from whatever devious plan he had, but she didn't know if he was capable enough of returning.

Feeling watched, Garnet rose. "Turn down the wick."

"But then we can't see anything. We can't see him coming for us."

"He can see us all the better with all this light." She started toward the cabin, hating the uncertainty. Had she made matters better or worse?

When they reached the cabin, she bolted the door and stayed up all night, listening in the dark for the man's return. He never came, not when a pack of wolves howled nearby, out on a hunt. And not when dawn chased the darkness away and brought light to the world.

* * *

Wyatt had better things to do than to traipse across the Rocky Mountains looking for a cheat and a liar. If he caught up to Eugene Jones, Wyatt was going to toss the old good-for-nothing fake in jail. Let him cool his heels and think about what he'd done.

After all, it was Eugene's fault Wyatt wasn't home tracking down the man who killed his brother. Ben had been a gentle soul with dreams of a better life when the gold rush struck. He'd left his job and home, since he had no family to tie him down, and gambled on finding a rich strike, just as thousands of other men did.

Wyatt squinted against the rising sun. He'd been riding all night, following a trail he feared would grow cold any second. He hated losing valuable time on his murder investigation. He also hated leaving Garnet alone in his cabin unprotected. He'd offered her a gun and she'd refused, no matter how he pressed.

Remembering how her chin had set with a stubborn determination touched him now, pulling him from dark thoughts. How he'd enjoyed the times their fingers had brushed. His blood thrummed just thinking of it, of how fragrant her skin was, sweet like satin, rich like silk.

What was wrong with him? Wyatt tried to shake those images from his head. He ought to be alert and concerned about his own hide, riding through this rugged wilderness, but he was thinking of her. Porcelain-fine skin. A luxurious cascade of ebony hair. A spark of integrity in blue-green eyes.

Hell, he didn't deserve a woman like her. Hadn't he learned his lesson? Hadn't his divorce taught him that a decent, proper lady didn't want a man like him? Garnet had been unbending in her refusal to even touch a loaded gun, much less keep one with her in his absence.

What did that tell him? She'd explained to him how she deplored violence of any kind. And he was a man who made his living on the violent side of life. Despite her toughness and her independent ways, he'd bet the entire yield of Ben's claim that she could never stomach the true Wyatt Tanner, deputy marshal.

There was the town of Cedar Heights in the distance. Wyatt pushed his tired horse into an easy lope down the trail, kicking up great plumes of dust. Morning birdsong punctuated the air as he rode down the main street. He checked at the only hotel in town—a seedy, disreputable establishment. Luckily the proprietor owed him a favor and agreed to open up early so they could talk.

No man matching Eugene Jones's description had spent the night in his hotel, but he had eaten at the diner. The wife remembered the old man bragging how he was going to catch the stage to Feddington, a town just across the Canadian border. Wyatt hired a fresh horse at the livery and rode after the stage. He caught it around noon, its axle broken on a rugged mountain pass. It had been robbed, and Eugene had lost the last of Garnet's money . . . that is, what he hadn't spent in the gambling halls along the way.

CHAPTER SIX

It wasn't fair that Pa was gone, and now she was stuck with Garnet, who was mad as a wet hornet. Wiping the tears from her eyes, Golda padded carefully around the back corner of the shack. With all the dust that rose with each dainty step, she knew it was useless to try to keep her new pale pink dimity gown from becoming dirty, but she did want to try. Even in the wilderness, a lady ought to care about her appearance.

Something rustled in the bushes, sounding sharp and dangerous, and then a shadow struck out from behind the dense foliage. Golda remembered the trouble two nights ago and choked on a scream, then relaxed when she recognized him. The man who stood before her in the brilliant sunlight was Mr. Lance Lowell.

How handsome he was with broad shoulders and a sturdy look to his well-framed body. He was a bit lean, but time had yet to broaden him more. He smiled, and his round boyish face turned darling and captivated her.

She placed her hand over her breast to still her quick-beating heart. "Oh, Lance, I mean, Mr. Lowell. How perfectly lovely to see you again."

"I had to come." As if nervous, the handsome man tugged off his battered hat and held it by the tattered brim. "I heard about yer pa runnin' off in the night. I heard tell how Mr. Tanner searched every saloon and brothel in these parts for him. 'Bout tore the town apart."

"I know. He just got back." Golda's heavy sigh was nothing like the burden put upon her these days. "Garnet has been so unbearable and furious at Pa she can hardly slip a word from between her clenched teeth. And Mr. Tanner is positively terrifying."

"He's a dangerous man and oughtn't be anywheres near a lady as delicate as you."

Sincerity shone in his eyes and rang innocent in his voice, and Golda could not summon up one of Garnet's many lectures on the flaws of the male sex. Not a single one.

"It ain't right," he went on to say, "you bein' forced to stay in his cabin."

"I absolutely agree." Golda lifted a hand to fluff the curling tendrils around her face. She sensed that Lance had a kind heart, as kind as dear Pa's. "Oh, Lance, I feel so much safer now that you've paid me a visit."

"I got somethin' for ya." He reached inside his breast pocket and deposited a small drawstring bag onto her palm. "It ain't much, but it's all I got and I want ya to have it."

"Oh, Lance." Golda knew at once it was the gold he had panned from the creek with his own strong hands.

"You'll be needin' a stage ticket." Lance squared his shoulders proudly. "I mean to help you out."

"I have never heard of anything so noble or so selfless." And indeed, Golda never had. Her pa, no matter how she loved him, had never given her half as much. And as for Garnet, she was always too busy working day in and day out as a schoolteacher and on the farm. "You're a gallant gentleman."

Mr. Lance Lowell, despite his battered dusty clothes, did indeed look like a flesh-and-blood hero to Golda's eyes. There was such a dependable responsibility in the way he held his shoulders and in the determined, manly set of his chin. Her heart fluttered. She hadn't had the opportunity to actually meet many men, but she couldn't help but believe Lance was so different than the type of men Garnet had warned her about.

Anyone could see the burn of kindness in his gentle eyes. Anyone could see how he took on burdens not his own.

Golda stared down at the small string poke, plump in her palm. She knew the value of the dust within would undoubtedly be small, but it was the thought that mattered. Perhaps there might be enough to purchase two stagecoach tickets out of town. Then Garnet could quit her infernal fuming.

But staring up into Lance's eyes, so soft and warm like melted fudge on the stove, Golda suddenly felt deeply sad at the thought of leaving. She had never met such a man as Lance Lowell and she didn't wish to leave him.

"We've missed the morning stage. I'm afraid we shall be stranded here in Stinking Creek for an entire week, until the next stage." Now she was almost glad.

"I know." Lance gripped his battered hat more tightly. "I hate for ya to go, but it ain't right for ya to be stranded here."

Golda's heart swelled. His selfless statement only proved his worth as a man. He gave her this gold knowing she would leave town with it. She dared to meet his gaze, a bold move for which Garnet would admonish her if she knew.

"Perhaps you might come visit me before I leave?"

A broad grin split the boyish handsomeness of Lance's round face. "I'd be mighty pleased to do that, Miss Golda. I was hopin' maybe you might ask me to visit."

Hope began to grow so tightly in her chest that it hurt, but Golda didn't mind. She had never felt so joyful, so alive.

For the first time in her life she had a beau. A man who clearly adored her, and who just might in time fall deeply in love with her.

Golda's heart swelled, right along with her most secret dreams.

"Mr. Lowell," she said now in greatest confidence, "I would welcome a visit from you any time at all."

* * *

"*No!* Absolutely not."

Garnet stormed across the cabin. She had never felt such furious rage in all her life than she did now at Wyatt Tanner's offer.

Not even at her pa, who'd duped her over and over again, had made her as angry as the man standing before her, whose dependable presence was like the steady beam of the sun above.

"Just take the damn gold," he ground out with sizable frustration. He hauled out the cabin's only chair and settled down to the table, looking dusty and trail-weary. "I can always pan more from the creek where I got it."

"But it's your life's savings." Garnet whirled around and stared at the man who reclined so casually in that crude chair. A new bottle of whisky winked in the sunshine that streamed through the yawning door. "I won't leave you as penniless as Pa left me."

"Trust me, I won't be penniless." Wyatt cracked open the seal on the bottle. "I have a gold claim. With gold on it. All it takes is a little work."

"*If* there is gold." Garnet crossed her arms. "I can't do it. I can't even consider it. I won't take your money, Wyatt."

"Give me one good reason why not."

"I've got my pride." She felt strung tight as a clothesline, ready to snap. "I've always fended for myself. And I'm not about to start relying on others to see to my needs."

"Oh, so that's it." He dared to chuckle. Clearly, he liked to live dangerously. "You're too proud a woman to take money from a man like me."

Garnet raised her chin a notch, her stance unyielding. "I have never needed a man's money, and I never will. I am capable of taking care of myself."

"How are you going to do that? Get yourself a patch of land and pan for gold?"

"Pan for gold? Goodness, I'll not resort to such unindustrious work. Surely there has to be some sort of respectable wage I can earn in this town."

And yet, even as she made the statement, she pictured Stinking Creek as it was the night she arrived. Scandalous. Dangerous. Sinful.

"The only respectable wages you could make are in the brothel." Wyatt tipped his head back and took three long pulls from the whiskey bottle. His throat worked with each swallow.

A brothel! "Is that what you think a woman is good for? A man's sport?" Oh, she'd had nearly enough of him, even if he had tried to rescue her savings from Pa. Furious beyond all measure, she stomped over to the table and wrapped her fingers around the neck of the whiskey bottle. She wished it was *his* neck.

"Hey! That's not what I meant at all. Garnet, give me back my booze."

He bounced up so quickly his chair tumbled backward onto the dirt floor, but she gave the bottle a good toss before he could stop her. She watched the whiskey fly through the air end over end, alcohol spilling like rain. The bottle hit a thin tree and thunked to the ground, broken and empty.

Garnet's chest swelled with satisfaction.

He crowded beside her in the doorway and sighed with complete disappointment. "What in the hell did you do that for?"

Suddenly, she realized her mistake. Crowded together in the doorway, she turned to face him. They were improperly close. Nearly nose-to-nose. If she took a deep breath, her breasts would brush up against the soft cotton fabric of his shirt. Of his chest.

"Don't run off with another bottle of mine."

"Then don't drink in my presence."

"Lady, this is my house. I'll do whatever the hell I want." He pressed closer, close enough that his breath fanned her face. He smelled faintly of coffee and more powerfully of liquor. "If you don't like me, then I suggest you leave."

"Fine." Her chin firmed, but she wondered if she could hide the tears smarting in her eyes. "If you want, I'll pack our belongings and be on our way."

"With my gift of gold?"

"Wrong." Garnet felt the righteous anger spill out of her like flour from a sack. "I am beholden to no one."

"That's not entirely true. You stayed in my shack," he reminded her with a teasing grin. "That makes you beholden to me."

"And I greatly regret it," she admitted, trying not to laugh at him. The sparkle of humor brightening his eyes was contagious. Could she hold back her smile?

No. One quirked along her mouth, but he stepped away before it could change the tension between them. Garnet squinted in the too-bright sunshine. Inside the cabin she heard a clink of glass.

"Please, take the gold." He returned with a new bottle of whiskey. He broke the seal with the slightest pressure from his big hand. "I insist. Don't think of it as charity. Consider it incentive to leave my cabin and never come back." He winked.

"You want to pay me to leave you alone?"

"Yes." Wyatt tipped the bottle and drank deeply. "Why do you think I live out here in the wilderness where there are no women?"

"So you don't have to bathe?" He wasn't the only one who could tease.

"So I can have some peace and quiet." He leaned against the wall, half in shadow, half in light, and took another pull on the bottle. Whiskey burned down his throat. "Take the money, Garnet. You can't stay here."

Not when he had a job to do, a cover to protect. Everyone in this town thought he was a miner panning for gold. And in order to find his brother's killer, everyone had to believe it. He couldn't have a woman hanging around, especially not one as sharp-eyed and intelligent as Garnet Jones.

"Don't worry. You want peace and quiet, you will have it." She snatched up an empty bucket and strode off. The sunshine played in her rich black hair, and her fast feet kicked up a growing plume of dust. From the looks of it, her leg was healing nicely.

Wyatt watched her disappear toward the creek. Amazing. She meant what she said. She wasn't going to take his gold.

Wyatt tipped back the bottle and let the fire-hot liquid burn a river down his throat to his belly. He was a man who thought he'd seen everything. The beauty of the wilderness. Indians in battle. Outlaws so cold and soulless that it was enough to make a man believe in evil. And yet, this was a first. A woman who wouldn't take a man's money.

He had never heard of such a thing. He had never believed that such a woman lived.

Unable to douse his curiosity, Wyatt followed her to the creek. Garnet sat on a large round boulder at the water's edge, her skirts carefully tucked out of the water's reach. The wind tugged at the long fall of hair neatly bound at the base of her neck. Small curls caught the breeze and shivered.

As if she was aware of his eyes on her, Garnet turned.

"Did you come to offer me even more money so I will leave you alone?"

"I'm afraid to." He crossed his arms across his chest, casually resting the bottle between two fingers. "You have quite a temper."

"One of the reasons no man would ever marry me." She watched the gurgling creek.

She was a small woman. She might be tall, but that only emphasized the slight build of her shoulders, the tiny width of her waist, and all her vulnerable beauty. She wore a plain butter-yellow dress today, a soft, muted color that made her seem delicate.

Wyatt knelt down beside the rock.

She gave him an apologetic shrug. "I'm sorry I insulted you. I know you were only trying to help me."

"Yes." He sucked down another swallow of whiskey. Then he offered her the bottle. "Want some?"

"No." But she smiled. "I'm sorry I broke your other bottle."

"You just wanted someone to lash out at since your father isn't here." Wyatt found a small pebble and tossed it into the creek. The lazy waters swallowed the stone with a mild *kerplunk*.

Garnet sighed. "I know I'm not so easy to get along with. It's no secret that men dislike me. I'm the only spinster in Willow Hollow who has never had one gentleman caller, let alone a marriage proposal."

Wyatt stared at the creek. "Willow Hollow sounds like a place full of stupid men. They don't know a good woman when they see one."

"Yes." Garnet gazed at him carefully. Then her smile widened. "That's what I've always thought."

But Wyatt heard the slightest tremor in her voice and recognized the hollow sound of her words. Garnet wasn't tough like she pretended to be. He didn't have to be a genius to read the hurt in her eyes.

"I admit I've been a little difficult, and I must apologize," she said now. "I'm just shouldering so many worries. How will I get home? What if I don't return in time to start my winter term? And it isn't just my job I stand to lose. I can only hope Opal and Silver have done the preserving correctly. And the harvest. Ruby's husband agreed to put up the crop."

Wyatt tipped back his head and laughed. "Your sisters are named after gemstones?"

An answering smirk softened the worry lines around her lush mouth. "Yes, what's wrong with that?"

"Nothing."

"What else would a man obsessed with uncovering the earth's treasures name his daughters?"

Wyatt tried to picture his old man, the perpetual drunk, naming his sons in a like fashion. What type of drink might he be named after? What brand of whiskey? Or ale? Perhaps it was his own whiskey knocking giddiness into his blood, but Wyatt laughed hard and carefree for the first time in years.

"I don't appreciate you laughing at my expense," she scolded, but her eyes were laughing. "Does this mean you wouldn't mind if we stayed?"

"Oh, no. That's not possible."

"But—"

"Garnet. Staying here will not solve your problems. You said you needed to get home."

"I do. But I also need money."

"Look." He held out a small drawstring poke. "It's gold. And it's yours. My gift to you, not charity."

"Why? Wait, I know. Because you want me to leave."

But his reasons had changed. "Because you are the only person I've met in a long time who doesn't want something from me. I admire you for it, and I think you deserve a little help."

She smiled, deciding she liked the color of his eyes . . . and much, much more. "Oh, Wyatt. That's the nicest thing any man has ever said to me."

Wyatt set down his whiskey bottle. "I won't go that far."

She smiled, and it touched her face with a gentle beauty that surprised him. "I've never had anyone to talk over my troubles with. I was always the oldest and Ma was always so ill. I had to make all the decisions myself. I have always been so lonely. Thank you for being the one I can turn to. All we need is a roof over our heads, and your cabin is small and I have not worked out the details, but—"

"You're *staying*?" he interrupted again.

"You said you would help me."

"Yes, but—" Caught in his own trap, he sat there, searching for a way out. "I didn't mean for you to . . . I don't want you to . . . No. Absolutely not. I can't keep . . ."

Garnet's gaze fastened on his with the color of hope.

He felt that hope like a lead weight at the end of a pulley, dragging him closer to some place he didn't want to be. But how could he turn them out on the street?

"You can stay," he managed through a strangled throat. "But don't go giving me any grief. I'm not about to tidy up this place for you. This is my home. I know it's not good enough for you, but it will have to do until you find other accommodations, understood?"

He tried to add the harsh bite of anger to his voice that he'd perfected as a lawman. But it eluded him now as he watched the gratitude warm Garnet's face like a touch of morning sun.

Like a fool, he gave her a small smile. Not a big one. Not one reaching to his eyes or right from his heart, but still, even a small smile was the wrong thing to do. Garnet's defenses fell like a loose woman's drawers. She smiled, a pretty movement of her mouth. He could not look away.

"Thank you, Mr. Tanner." Her voice sounded light, as light as the dust shivering weightless in the air between them. "You don't know how I've been worrying what to do, where to go. I'm afraid for our safety in a town like this, and your cabin is more than good enough for me."

"It's a crude shanty with a dirt floor."

"I can live with a dirt floor." She shrugged, truly not minding. "Your cabin may be a little on the rough side, but you're mistaken if you think I'm used to luxuries. I've always just scraped by and made do and never had much of anything. I can take care of myself, but I can't protect us from dangerous men. I hate to ask you, but—" Her chin dipped, and lovely black ringlets fell across her brow. "Someone was in your stable the night you left."

"What?" He bolted forward, grabbing hold of her arm. "Who? Someone from town?"

"I don't know. I hit him in the head with one of your whiskey bottles."

"You what?" Wyatt couldn't believe it. "He threatened you? Tried to attack you?"

"No, but I figured he could, so I decided to act." She tilted her face up to his, and he could see the fear in her eyes, and the courage, too. "He got away before I could find out who he was or what he wanted. I was afraid I'd killed him, but I think I just cut his head pretty bad."

Wyatt thought about that. If Ben's killer saw him leave town to hunt down Eugene, then he might have thought the claim would be abandoned and he'd be free to keep searching for Ben's stash of gold. Hell, he could have stumbled on Garnet and hurt her.

He hauled her into his arms, driven by concern. "Are you all right? You can't trust the men in these parts, Garnet. They are a rough sort. Outlaws and criminals. Even murderers."

"That's why I would like to stay with you as long as it's necessary. I know you'll keep us safe, Wyatt, and that's all that matters."

Although she spoke like a prim spinster, there was something different in her voice, something changed in her eyes.

He'd seen that something before, and it shook him straight down to his heart. That sparkle of interest, that allure of attraction. It couldn't be true. Garnet Jones didn't like men like him.

He had to be imagining it.

CHAPTER SEVEN

When Wyatt ambled home for supper after searching the entire forest for signs of the man Garnet hurt, it was with a stiff back and aching joints. At least he had footprints this time. Sure evidence that the murderer wasn't a prospector. No cheap work boots made the few tracks left behind in the dust. They had to be fine expensive shoes, the kind the merchants and gambling hall owners wore. The footprints revealed that the shoes' owner had average-sized feet and was limping slightly, as if he'd been injured before his confrontation with Garnet. Perhaps on the road when she arrived.

Exhaustion hung about his head like fog, and the strong rays of the late day sun burned his eyes. He needed to go to town and check up on these leads while they were fresh, while the killer was still sporting his wounds.

As he neared his cabin, his brother Ben's cabin, he saw the light gray plume of smoke lifting from the stovepipe above the canvas roof. The women were probably cooking supper, he considered, and his empty stomach growled as loudly as a bear. His mouth watered at the memory of Garnet's pancakes. Fluffy and moist, spongy and light. Maple syrup sweetening the stack like spun sugar. Yes, it wouldn't be such a bad thing to have himself some of those pancakes right about now.

Instead of marching directly through the cabin's only door, he skirted the corner and headed toward the privy. Finding new clues that would lead him straight to the killer had put him in a great mood. But the minute he reached the back corner of his cabin and saw what Garnet had done, that good mood suffered a miserable death.

She'd strung perfectly good rope from the corner of the shack to the tree in the fashion of a clothesline. Dripping wet, lye-scented wool blankets were draped over the rope, neat end to neat end.

As far as Wyatt could tell, it was every blanket he owned.

A horrible anger began to boil like hot water through his veins. Something like a windstorm swept through his brain, and he marched back to the cabin, trying to gain control of his spiraling temper.

He threw open the door and froze at an even more upsetting sight. His only two buckets sat on the top of the stove, full of bubbling water. He could see the steam from where he stood. Young Lance Lowell's wash tub was in the middle of the room, full of lye soap. Garnet knelt before it, arms submerged up to her elbows.

Piles of something sat in the tub. He could see the wet lengths of fabric darkening the wash water.

Wyatt stepped forward. "*What in the hell are you doing?* "

She looked up from her work. "Clearly I am doing laundry."

"You washed my blankets. You washed every single one of my blankets. Wasn't my coffeepot enough for you?"

He marched over to the washtub and dared to reach into the sudsy, foul-smelling water. His fingers snagged a wet length of wool and he lifted it up. A sodden, dripping blanket.

Wyatt swore and dropped it back into the tub. Water splashed everywhere, wetting great patches of his trousers. Garnet hopped backward, having been splashed, too.

"I washed your stove, but you haven't noticed that yet. I'd never seen such a filthy stove." She stared up at him with angry eyes. "I wanted to do this for you since you're allowing us to stay here. I might not be able to pay rent, but I can make myself useful. I can't tell you how dirty everything is around here. You probably don't have the slightest idea because you've become accustomed to the filth."

"Did you ever stop and think that maybe I like my blankets this way?" Wyatt stormed across the room. The girl, Golda, gasped at his approach and shrank back into the corner, eyes round with terror.

"What about your clothes?" Garnet crooked an eyebrow at him. "I thought—"

"*What about my clothes?*" he growled.

She opened her mouth, but no more words came out.

Something else was wrong. He felt a tight tingle of wariness slip down his spine. "Tell me right now. What did you do with my clothes?"

"I washed them, too. They're soaking in the rinse water. They need a lot of soaking."

"Are all my clothes in there?" Hell, he didn't deserve this, this *civilized* need to clean everything that wasn't nailed down.

"All but your underthings," Garnet said in a quiet, embarrassed voice.

At least some of his possessions had escaped her lye soap. "Don't touch them, you hear?"

"I said they weren't in the rinse water. Your drawers are boiling in the bucket on the stove."

He closed his eyes, struggling not to lose his temper. "I'm going to fetch wood for the fire. I'm hungry."

Wyatt looked mad. Garnet left the shirt to soak and stood. "Let me cook for you."

"Fine." He stormed from the room, leaving them alone.

Well, she didn't like this arrangement either, but what choice did she have? When Wyatt had offered his help, she had to accept it. Did he think she relied on men all the time? Did he think she just took what she wanted every day from any man she met, even if it was an entire house?

No, and he ought to know that. It hurt her pride terribly that she was forced to depend on him now. She, the feared schoolmarm of Willow Hollow, had never failed to be self-reliant before now.

Pa had done this to her. That no-account man cared more about his own recreating than he ever would his daughters. And Wyatt was a miner too, just like Pa. He drank whiskey and panned for gold. She had to believe he was no different in nature.

Yet she knew he was different. Her chest constricted, and it was hard 'to breathe. She shouldn't group Wyatt in the same category of men as Pa. Wyatt helped others. He may not be perfectly tidy, but he had tended her wound, comforted her, and given her his bed when she had no other place to sleep.

And most of all, he had never lied to her about the kind of man he was.

Golda's footsteps tapped close across the wood floor, skirting the rinse barrel. "I've something to tell you, but first you have to promise not to get angry. You know you have a temper."

"A temper?" It was true, so Garnet couldn't argue. She braced herself for the worst. "What exactly have you done now that will set off my temper?"

"Oh, nothing I've done. Not exactly." Golda didn't seem so sure of herself. She looked helpless and muddled and pressed a nervous hand to her chest as if a guilty heart beat within. "I just want you to promise, first."

"Promise?" Garnet grabbed a towel to dry her hands. "I make no promises. Tell me what you've done."

"Oh, Garnet." Troubled, Golda hung her head. She fiddled around in her small reticule and produced a leather pouch.

Garnet recognized it at once. Drawstring pokes fashioned from tanned leather were notorious purses for prospector's silly dust. Shock rocked through her. "You've stolen Mr. Tanner's gold!"

Golda's head came up. "I did not. Really, Garnet, I would never steal. Mr. Lowell dropped by to visit and he gave this to me."

"Mr. Lowell? He came by to see you? When?" Garnet sighed. This was very bad news indeed. "I didn't hear his knock at the door."

"Well," Golda hesitated, as if she knew darn good and well the truth would only make matters worse. "He didn't exactly knock at the door. He was waiting in the bushes for me to come outside."

"Oh, a proper sort of gentleman."

"But he is!" Golda rose to an immediate defense. "He wanted me to have all of his gold even if it takes me away from him. Isn't he gallant? Isn't he noble?"

A horrible pounding beat through Garnet's head. "*Give it back to him at once.*"

"What?" Innocent-eyed, Golda stared at her sister. "But—"

"Give it back, I said." Garnet saw only disaster. A disaster her younger sister did not understand, could not. She had been too young to remember Ma dying of a broken heart, pining for the one man who could never love her. "You will not be beholden to that man for whatever minuscule amount of dust he's actually managed to pan from that muddy creek."

"How can you be so ungrateful?" Golda cried out. "Lance is kind and noble and generous. He worked hard for this gold."

"It's highly improper to call such a man by his first name." This couldn't be happening, Garnet thought, beginning to panic. This was just the way Ma had always described how she fell in love with Pa. The bumbling miner, young and handsome, had a kindness that had lured poor unsuspecting Ma into a life of poverty and desperate unhappiness. "Come with me, we shall return that gold dust immediately and all will be set right."

"*No.*" Golda planted her feet. Defiance shone in her eyes. "I won't be as hateful as you, Garnet. I won't. Lance—I mean Mr. Lowell—was wonderful to me and I—"

The door banged open. Wyatt filled the threshold, all flesh-and-blood man made of powerful muscle and iron will. Golda trembled at his presence, but Garnet felt her anger drain like water from a spigot. Her gaze met his and her heart drummed, her burdens felt lighter.

Good Lord, it wasn't the same, this admiration she felt for Wyatt Tanner. It wasn't at all the same mistake Ma had made in coming to like, then love, then marry Pa. And it certainly wasn't anything like the terrible judgment Golda was showing toward Lance Lowell.

Why, she didn't even like Wyatt Tanner. And as long as she refused to like him, then she didn't need to worry about falling victim to love.

* * *

The next day, Wyatt had agreed to walk her and Golda into town and serve as protection. Garnet's first goal was of course to make sure Mr. Lance Lowell received all of his gold dust. Then she would need money both for immediate needs like groceries and future needs like stage tickets. That meant she would have to secure a respectable job.

"Too bad there are no children here," she mused. "I am a fine schoolteacher."

"A few of the women in town have kids." Wyatt walked at her side, shortening his long stride, perhaps out of consideration for her shorter step and injured leg. Garnet tried not to think about what a thoughtful man he was.

"I did not know there were other women in this town."

"There are brothels, you know. Women live and work in those."

Garnet blushed. "I was unaware that soiled doves were referred to as women."

"Well, they are all the same to me." Wyatt shrugged. "When I was a sheriff, I never gave the molls a hard time. They were just working for their living, same as me.

"*You* were a sheriff?" That made her laugh. "I can't picture you with a tin badge on your chest."

"Why not?"

"Miners don't hold respectable jobs."

"I have my moments of responsibility."

When she thought about it, she could imagine him in lawman's garb. He would look strong and capable and so handsome, women had probably fallen at his feet. "When you were a sheriff, I hope you washed your things more often."

"What is your obsession with cleaning? I don't think it's healthy to be too clean."

"Stop teasing me. At least I am not as slothful as to allow my person to smell like a dead skunk from twenty yards away."

"I don't smell like a skunk."

"No, you don't." He smelled wonderful, fresh as the forest, and it was wrong of her to notice.

"Besides, this is uncivilized country. If word got around that I scrubbed house and ironed my sheets I'd be laughed right out of town."

Golda, apparently recovered sufficiently from her bit of the sulks, snorted in what sounded like disgust.

Garnet said nothing, determined not to give notice to this silly notion her baby sister harbored over young Lance Lowell's gallantry. She had never met a truly gallant man, one who had given something freely to a woman without wanting something in return, except of course for the singular example of Wyatt Tanner.

Perhaps because he had saved her, been the kind of man at heart that her pa was not. When she was her most vulnerable, hurt and betrayed, Wyatt had helped her. He rode after Pa and tracked him down, even if he had recovered no money from the gambling old man. He'd even had him thrown in jail for a few nights, just to think about his misdeeds. And now Wyatt was keeping her safe as he escorted her to town. He'd stood by her far more often than any one person ever had.

Not that she needed to lean on anyone for long.

She could smell town before she actually saw it. A disagreeable odor wafted on the brisk afternoon wind; yet it was the sight of the town in broad daylight that offended her more. Numerous tents were scattered along the wide, flat stretch of the yellow-brown riverbank, crowded together in various states of repair. Unwashed clothing and bedding could be viewed from some of the open flaps, as well as the sleeping men inside.

Unpainted buildings marched in a long line down the dirt street. Saloons emitted the sound of random gunfire, men's brazen shouts, and tinny piano music. In the brothels, many brightly dressed women stood in plain view, looking out the parlor windows or standing on the street smoking cigars, all awaiting customers.

Garnet batted at a couple persistent flies. "Most men are walking around in their underwear."

"The brutes," Wyatt teased, his breath tickling her ear when he leaned close.

"I could have worn my chemise to town had I known underwear was the fashion."

That made him laugh, and she was glad. Garnet knew she was out of her element here. She thought of the pleasant town back home, of its clean streets and friendly shops. Fresh green trees hugged the lane, giving way to neatly kept little houses and freshly painted storefronts and the niceties of churches and schools. How her heart ached for home.

"Garnet," Golda squeaked. "Strange men are looking at us."

They were. The men riding down Main Street stopped their horses to stare. Windows in the saloons and gaming halls filled with curious faces. Men climbed out of their tents wearing only bright red union suits and watched, bottles in hand.

As they progressed down the street, Garnet had never felt this uncomfortable. The whole town stood silent, staring at the three of them. She felt like a spectacle, like a tropical bird lost in this foreign yellow-brown country.

She was also intensely aware of Wyatt's hands edging toward the walnut grips of his holstered revolvers.

"Here's the general store," he said in a low voice, not daring to look at her.

"I'll go in here and offer my services to the shopkeeper," Garnet decided. Her hand shook, but she was determined to still it. "I'm excellent at mathematics and meticulous at record-keeping. Perhaps they can use help."

Wyatt fought a smile. "If you need a recommendation, I'll be happy to tell any prospective employer how well you scrubbed my drawers."

That man! Garnet blushed. "Since you think you're so funny, I'm going to send you to locate young Mr. Lowell's tent and chaperone Golda. That will teach you to make wisecracks in my company."

Wyatt lifted one brow, silently laughing. "That's a cruel punishment."

"I know." Warmth glittered inside her, and she bit her cheek to keep from chuckling in the middle of town. "Golda intends to return Lance's meager amount of gold dust. Please see that she does so."

"But Garnet." Golda's bottom lip pulled into a deeper pout. "We ought to keep the gold. Perhaps it will be useful for our journey home."

"A respectable lady does not accept gifts from a man, especially one she does not know." Red-hot anger burned in her chest, anger at Golda's stubborn refusal to admit her folly. "Return that measly dust. Then come join me in the general store. We must secure employment."

"But I've never had to work before."

"Perhaps it's high time. I fear you've been spoiled terribly by all of us, and only now the ill effects are starting to show."

"That's unfair," Golda frowned, puckering up her pretty face. High red color of what could only be anger burned across her cheeks. "I am to go to college next fall and study music."

"Not if we can't raise enough money to buy seats on the next stage out of here."

"Ma'am?" A rail-thin, rawboned man stepped forward. A thin mustache lined his upper lip, hopping when he spoke. His gray eyes were kind as he took off his hat nervously. "Couldn't help overhearin' yer problem. I sure would be happy ta give ya my gold. Don't know if it would be enough, though."

Garnet stared at the ungroomed stranger and saw only the honest intention to help. "It's very kind of you, sir, but I couldn't accept."

"Why not? T'would be no trouble a'tall," the man assured her.

"I would consider it an honor helpin' out two fine ladies such as yerselves."

How kind. Of course, Pa was kind, too, when he wanted something. "Thank you very much, but it wouldn't be proper for us to take your gold."

Aware of the skinny man's downcast look but at a loss as to how to fix it, she caught Wyatt's gaze. He held out his hand and she took it. Her skin heated when their palms touched. He accompanied her up the stairs, then opened the glass door for her. She basked in his protective presence, in the warmth of his smile.

"Don't worry. No one will harm you while I'm here." He tipped his hat back, revealing his eyes. Something wondrous burned there, an emotion inviting and real.

Could it be? Did he care for her? Garnet's heart squeezed. How she wanted to see more of that emotion shine in his beautiful dark eyes. How she wished . . . well, she wished for many things that would never come true. And this one wouldn't either. A man as handsome as Wyatt Tanner would hardly desire her.

Her heart felt raw and aching.

"I expect some kind of repayment for accompanying your sister today." Wyatt managed a smile, and it softened his chiseled face, making her see past the plain miner's garb to the man of substance beneath.

"I will reward you appropriately for the torture." She smiled in spite of herself. It wasn't fair to find humor in her sister's broken heart, but she did appreciate Wyatt's sacrifice. She suspected he didn't like Golda.

Before she could bask in his presence any longer, Wyatt tipped his hat to her and strode away. She ached to turn around and watch him go, all strong shoulders and powerful stride. Instead she stepped inside the store and squinted in the dark interior.

"You wouldn't be one of the ladies staying over at Tanner's place, would you?" a gregarious male voice boomed out directly behind her ear.

Garnet jumped, knocking over a shovel. The tool clattered to a noisy end on the dusty wood floor. She knelt quickly to retrieve the item, embarrassed by her clumsiness, when a large, attractive, and clean-looking male hand reached out and closed gently around the shovel's wooden handle.

Garnet gazed up into the face of a well-kept, clean-shaven,

clean-smelling man. The shopkeeper offered a civilized smile, but he didn't bother to move away from her.

"I see the rumors are true. There is a pretty lady living on the outskirts of town," he said with a flash of white, well-brushed teeth. "Aren't I lucky my father sent me here to set up a store?"

A blush crept up her neck. He was entirely too close. And she didn't like it. So she stepped away.

"Let me formally introduce myself," he continued, stepping closer, with a slight limp. "I'm Barrett Carson, general partner. My father and my brothers own several stores throughout this little corner of Montana."

Garnet blinked. She wasn't impressed. Oh, sure, she could recognize the glint in his eyes, the warm lure in his voice, the charm in his speech as he tried to impress her. She could recognize a man's courting ways.

Nothing on this earth could be quite so dangerous.

Garnet set her chin. "I've come to inquire after employment," she said now, more than willing for a change of subject. "I am an exceedingly diligent worker. Are you hiring?"

"Well, no." Mr. Carson shook his head, scattering an attractive collection of hair. "There isn't enough business to warrant another employee, but I could use some woman's work around here. Just look at the way the dust has accumulated on my shelves."

Garnet did not bother to hide her frown. "I could be persuaded to clean for you. I have cleaned house all my life. I am exceedingly efficient at scrubbing, you know. I'm sorry to point this out, but your floors are a dreadful sight. Might you want them cleaned as well?"

Mr. Carson agreed with a charming smile.

Garnet turned their conversation to services needing to be performed. In no time at all she had effectively talked him into a very pleasing wage.

* * *

Wyatt rescued the last of his clothes from the shanty. He was moving into the stable. The stable was proving to be a better refuge than he first thought. Garnet hadn't thought to come and scrub it down, for one thing. Golda wasn't there, clucking in fear of his presence like a chicken on butchering day.

Yes, Wyatt had peace and quiet to work out his leads, to think about his accumulating evidence. Besides, he'd rather share his life with a horse. His mare didn't leave him puzzled and confused and wanting something he couldn't have.

Just looking at Garnet across the length of the cabin was about all he could take. She was humming some cheerful little song, a pleasant tune that made him want to hear more. Having taken foodstuffs on credit from Carson's general store, she was frying up a salt pork and egg meal. The aroma made his mouth water.

Did she thank him for protecting her in town today? No. Did she thank him for escorting her empty-headed, manipulative little sister to Lowell's tent? No. Did she thank him for keeping the men in town from salivating all over her? No. She kept her back to him, humming that mesmerizing tune, happy with her good fortune over securing so many offers of employment.

Someone knocked at the open door.

Wyatt frowned, turning to face the newcomer. Probably another man from town, eager to see "Miss Garnet." Boy, didn't those offers just keep coming?

It had started with young Billy Bob offering Garnet and Golda use of his tent. Then, when the men learned of Garnet's new business, they had swarmed her in the street offering up their homes and businesses and clothes to be washed by a proper, experienced woman.

Garnet announced that any man could drop off a rucksack of laundry at the cabin. If they wanted complete cleaning services at their home, they could discuss such things at that time. Golda had not been happy to learn she would be expected to scrub those garments on the new washboard Garnet had purchased on credit from Carson's store.

Elmer Minks, the tall rawboned man who had politely offered his gold to Garnet, stood nervously outside the shack, his battered hat in hand.

Wyatt frowned at him. "What do you want?"

"Hear Miss Garnet is takin' in laundry." Elmer Minks's eyes lit with bright admiration when he said Garnet's name. "Now, I don't have a cabin to clean, bein' as I'm livin' in a tent. But tell Miss Garnet I do have me a mighty problem with my duds."

"You're not welcome here."

"Wyatt!" Garnet's sharp admonition rang through the cabin. She looked particularly attractive with the soft loose braid of her hair coiled artfully around her head, now that she had purchased hairpins from the store. The heat from the stove had steamed loose tendrils into soft gossamer curls that now framed her heart-shaped face. Worse, she looked even more pretty with pleasure alight in her blue-green eyes, the color as unusual and as striking as the woman herself.

It was his opinion that perhaps she ought to wait to speak to Elmer Minks until she looked less attractive.

Maybe in twenty years.

She crossed the cabin in two steps. "Hello, Mr. Minks. I remember your generous offer in town today. I hear you wish to hire me to do your laundry."

"Why, I'd be rightly honored, ma'am." Elmer's smile was bright enough to outshine the sun overhead.

Wyatt scowled. He had had enough of this nonsense. Men coming to the door with their filthy underwear, all smiling and putting on charm just to impress "Miss Garnet." Some even went so far as to shave.

Once again, she refused Elmer's generous offer of gold. It wasn't a lot of money, but judging by the size of that poke, it had to be a hundred dollars.

A woman who wouldn't take a man's money. It still amazed him. Especially since it didn't appear to be a family trait. Young Golda, who had stepped in to take over frying the salt pork, was still pouting. Her silence filled the shack despite Garnet's lively chatter. Above the promise of clean clothes by Friday and the fee of a dollar in gold, the girl's sullen mood reigned supreme.

Oh, Wyatt hadn't been fooled when he escorted the reluctant Golda to Lance's tent. He was certain she did not return the gold. And in truth, he didn't care. He'd been too busy watching every man he came across for a sign of a limp or a bandaged head. But too many men wore hats to tell for sure.

"I can't believe that." Garnet laid a hand on her throat, her eyes wide with astonishment as she closed the door. "Mr. Minks just proposed to me."

"*What?*" Golda dropped the spoon with a clatter. "*You* got a marriage proposal?"

"The second one today." Garnet nodded, clearly amused. "I have never received the slightest interest from a man in the first twenty-six years of my life. And now I've received two offers in the same day. It's astounding."

"It's shocking, that's what it is." Golda's plump little mouth tightened in an unattractive sneer. "You are too old for such attention. Those awful men are just trying to use you, Garnet. They are simply hungry for a woman's companionship and there are no other women around. They are giving you false hope."

"Oh." Garnet's step faltered.

Wyatt watched the bright gleam in her eyes dim and the smile fade from her soft mouth. For a brief moment she had looked young and so beautiful, a glimpse of her real self beneath all the burdens and responsibilities she took on so seriously and so bravely.

Wyatt's throat tightened and he stepped forward to chastise the girl, but already Garnet was talking in her typical no-nonsense fashion.

"I'm sure you're right." Garnet's step was heavier than before. "I'm sure those men are poor, misguided souls lacking a woman's helpful influence. They are so lonely that even I look appealing."

As if it didn't matter, as if her feelings weren't hurt, Garnet grabbed up a scrap of his old shirt to check the oven. Wyatt watched, his heart strung taught as a rope, not sure if it would hold or break. Garnet bent from her tiny waist and lowered the oven's lid. He watched the spare fabric of her skirt tighten across her behind.

Too much trouble, too bossy, too opinionated for the likes of him. And far too fine, courageous, and loyal.

Wyatt told himself it didn't matter that there was another knock at the door, another man eager to ask "Miss Garnet" to do his laundry. But it did.

CHAPTER EIGHT

It wasn't fair, that's what it was. Golda stood up from the washtub set beneath a tall tree's shade and stretched her stiff, aching back. She'd been working most of the evening, ever since Garnet insisted she help wash the supper dishes. Her back ached from bending over the wash-tubs. Her arms hurt from scrubbing men's dirty shirts against the washboard. Her knees hurt from kneeling in the dirt. Her normally soft, smooth hands might never recover from the harsh lye soap.

Golda left Elmer's shirts in the washwater and strolled the short distance in the shade to the creek. Her wet hands, red and wrinkled, dripped as she walked, leaving tiny droplets of mud in the ever-present dust. At least, if they earned enough money doing this awful work, they wouldn't have to stay here with Mr. Tanner. Maybe she could even talk Garnet into moving into town, so she would be closer to Lance.

She sat down on a rather large boulder and stared down at the lazy little creek. Fallen leaves floated down-stream with the current, leaves from trees that were already changing colors.

Oh, how wonderful it was to have visited with Lance the other day, despite the circumstance. Sure, that frightening Mr. Tanner had watched and listened nearly the entire time, but oh, just to see Lance's dear face. How handsome he was! Already she loved his boyish kindness, those friendly warm eyes and that charming smile.

Golda was so happy, she felt certain her heart might float up like one of those fluffy white clouds and set itself free in the sunset.

"I fear I'm a bit jealous," Lance had confessed in his tent while that nasty Mr. Tanner had stood just outside the open flap. "I used ta be the only man that knew you was here in town. I had you all to myself. But now everyone can see you, and see how downright beautiful ya are, and I fear you'll be smitten with a more dapper fella."

"Oh, no," she had been quick to assure him. She had swelled up with pride because Lance thought she was beautiful. Could a girl ask for anything more? "I'm not allowed to talk to any other men. Garnet has granted me permission to speak with you just this once."

"Yer sister's a bit . . . well, bossy, ain't she?" Lance had asked diplomatically.

"Oh," Golda had giggled; she couldn't help it. "She has been particularly unbearable lately. She spends entirely too much time with that Mr. Tanner."

Lance's eyes widened. "She ain't bein' neglectful to you, is she?"

Golda bit her lip. "She does intend to make me work like a slave."

"I've made up my mind, dearest," Lance said after great thought. "Wait for me outside Mr. Tanner's cabin in the evening."

"Oh, Lance." His name rolled off her tongue like the sweetest of candies. "I'll be waiting. But we mustn't let Garnet know."

Now, after several evenings had passed without one single sign of darling Lance, Golda felt sorely disappointed. She returned to her work, scrubbing diligently at the clothes that took a second washing to come clean. Then she heard the footsteps behind her and spun around expectantly, her heart in her throat.

It was only Garnet. "Did you remember to change the rinse water?"

"No. I've been too exhausted scrubbing these horrid shirts."

"Those horrid shirts are going to make us enough money to get home before snow flies," Garnet said in her superior way.

Golda hadn't quite noticed it before, but her sister's know-it-all attitude was really beginning to annoy her. Not that she didn't love Garnet or feel grateful. Garnet had been a mother to her, for heaven's sake. But now she was always harping on about how hard life was and how important it was to shoulder responsibilities. How dangerous men were and how worthless Pa was.

Well, Golda had never believed that about Pa, even now after he'd left them stranded here. She knew there had been a darn good reason why he had taken their money. And if their life's savings was something he needed that badly, then Golda was glad he helped himself to Garnet's reticule.

Garnet now glanced at the stack of unwashed clothes and eyed the line on which hung row after row of shirts. Her thin lips pressed together in a disagreeable frown.

"Golda, I'm sure you've done your best today, but you are going to have to work faster. We have a stack of laundry to get through, and when it's dry there's the ironing, don't forget."

Golda sighed. The task seemed unending, and she was certain Garnet was determined to kill her off with this awful, back-breaking drudgery.

"We'll work together on this tomorrow morning. Right now I want you to go inside and fry up the salt pork. Look, someone else has ridden up. I hope that's another new customer."

"Right." Golda held back the sneer until her sister was out of sight. She saw how eager Garnet was to find more shirts for her to scrub.

"*Psst.*"

Golda turned toward the trees. She recognized the handsome face peering out at her through the undergrowth. Her whole heart leapt with immeasurable joy, as endless as the sky overhead, as bright as all the stars wandering through the night.

"Is she gone?" Lance asked, cautiously gazing out at the yard.

"She's gone for *now*." Golda sighed. "Oh, Lance, it's *good* to see you."

"I have to know, darling Golda." Lance stepped out of the foliage and reached gallantly for her hand. "All the men in town can't stop talkin' about you and your sister. You are such a vision. Such a beautiful princess. I know I'm not good enough for such a fine lady."

"Why, don't put yourself down, Lance—Mr. Lowell," she said, charmed beyond the capacity to think. "You're a fine man. A man any lady would be proud to know."

"But am I good enough to be your husband?" he asked anxiously. There was no mistaking the love burning in his eyes. "Would ya marry me, Golda?"

* * *

Garnet eyed the freshly shaven man as he dismounted from his bay gelding. He looked neat and tidy, and he wore such nice shoes. He wasn't a prospector, like so many of the men in this territory, but probably a shop owner. She did spy a rucksack slung over the back of his saddle and excitement thrummed in her chest. More business! Goodness, in a month, if this kept up, she would have hopes of having enough money to head home.

"Good day, ma'am," the man politely tipped his hat. "The word in town is that you are starting a laundry business."

"Yes, sir. I'm also cleaning a few of the businesses in town. Mr. Carson's store and Mr. Busby's saloon and boardinghouse." The prostitute who'd tried to help her that frightening first night in town had approached her, too, asking to hire her. Garnet didn't think she ought to list a brothel as one of her jobs, especially when she only cleaned the living quarters for the girls and the parlor.

"I'm Gus Adams and I own the Lucky Day Gambling Hall. I could use someone with your talents. I pay my bartender to clean up, but he isn't so good at it. Would you be interested in cleaning for me?"

"Very much. I do have room in my schedule." Garnet was used to teaching school during the day and coming home to do the farm work. Such stamina would serve her well now.

"Good, then I would like to hire you." Gus had dark eyes that sparkled when he smiled. "I see you're stuck out here in Wyatt's cabin. He's not the most agreeable man in these parts."

"No, but he has been the perfect gentleman," Garnet confessed, not sure if Gus intended to slight Wyatt or compliment him. "He has offered us use of his cabin, although it's a terrible inconvenience to him."

"Yes, and so far from town." Gus's mouth twisted as he thought. "I have a cabin I normally rent, but the prospector left town a few weeks ago."

"You mean, it's vacant?" Hope sizzled in her heart. Not that she wanted to leave Wyatt, but if she had her own home, a place she paid for herself, why, she would be truly independent again. And no burden to the man she was beginning to care for way too much.

"Indeed." Gus's smile deepened. "In fact, I could offer the place in trade. It's a fine cabin, with a wood floor. For say, a weekly scrubbing of my gambling hall."

"No." Garnet's blood heated at the thrill of a negotiation. "How about two free weekly scrubbings? I guarantee you'll be pleased with my work. I'll need to view the cabin first, before I decide for certain."

"Of course. Stop by any time."

Goodness, this was going much better than she'd ever hoped. She then began negotiating a fair wage for laundry services.

* * *

G arnet pushed open the stable door with a great amount of trepidation in her heart. Her negotiations with Gus Adams had proven successful, but now she needed to ask Wyatt to take her to town. He'd made her swear she wouldn't head off alone, not after the incident the other night.

How would he act? Her chest squeezed. What if he were glad to be rid of them? That's how he would probably feel, and she wasn't certain if her heart could take the disappointment of not being wanted.

"Got yourself another client, huh?" Wyatt looked up from his marc's stall. The animal was grazing outside in the dappled twilight.

"You've made yourself a cozy place here." She saw the straw pallet he'd made himself, clean blankets heaped in a corner. A barrel of molasses served as a table, and a newspaper lay open on top of it, alongside an empty tin cup. A cut log served as a chair. "I bet you'd rather have your cabin back."

"What? Are you inviting me to move in with you?" Teasing humor flickered in his eyes, more alluring and attractive than Gus's pleasant sparkles, Garnet noted. Her stomach fluttered.

"No, I just thought maybe I should move to town. Maybe it would be better for my reputation and for your peace of mind to have us gone."

"*Gone?*" Wyatt bellowed with as much fury as if she had asked for his permission to set him on fire. "What gave you that harebrained idea?"

Garnet cringed, not expecting his anger. "You want us out of your cabin."

"No, I don't."

"You never wanted us to stay, Wyatt."

"Well, that was just . . . shock, that's all. The shock of having two women thrust into my life like that." He snatched up the pitchfork, gripping it between powerful hands. Obviously in a foul mood, he paraded over to the single stall and began disturbing the straw.

"You didn't seem shocked to me. And you were very angry when I washed your blankets and all your clothes."

"I was on the verge of losing my temper. You can't hold a man to his word at a time like that." Wyatt worked the soiled straw loose and began to stack it near the door. There was no mistaking the ripple of muscle beneath his cotton shirt.

Garnet tried to look somewhere else, but her gaze wandered back to watch his shirt stretch over his chest and shoulders with each movement. My, she was growing warm. Very warm.

But Wyatt seemed unaware of her physical state and simply continued mucking out the stall. He worked steadily without glancing up, as if looking at her would only ignite his temper more thoroughly. "Don't get me wrong I want you out of my place, off my land, out of my life. With all these men coming around, ruining my peace, having you leave this very second wouldn't be soon enough for me."

"Then why don't you want me to go?" Garnet asked, truly confused.

"Because . . ." He straightened from his work pitching straw. "Your bullet wound is not fully healed. And the fact that you're penniless. Both are my fault."

"Your fault?" He amazed her, he simply amazed her. All brawn and good looks, but he was more than that. He had a heart better than any man she had ever known. "I cannot see how Pa running off with my money is your fault."

"I didn't find him in time. He'd gambled and drunk away most of your savings. I would have taken it out of his hide, but he's an old man. I couldn't strike him. Other than letting him cool his heels in jail for a few days, there was nothing I could do."

He rubbed his brow with the back of his hand. "I never should have left him laying around on my cabin floor for so long. I suspected he was starting to be more healthy than he was pretending to be, but I let it pass."

"You aren't the first person Pa ever lied to."

"I know." So much warmth in that rum-smooth voice. "You don't deserve what he did to you, Garnet."

Little sparks of affection jumped to life in her heart, beautiful flames that warmed her entire chest and radiated through her body.

"It's nice to know you care."

"Of course I do. I feel responsible for you."

That warmth in her chest faded. Responsible? That's how he felt? The way an older brother felt for a sister? The way she felt for Golda? Garnet bowed her chin. Of course he didn't care for her. No man ever had, no man ever would.

Now there was no other decision to make. "I'm taking Gus up on his offer. He has a vacant cabin, and he offered me a reasonable rent. I can't continue to stay with you, now that I've secured employment and a home. I can't be beholden to you anymore."

"I see." Why did he sound disappointed?

"I've never had to depend on a man before," she explained. "And I can't continue to take advantage of you. You have allowed us to disrupt your life and eat your food and sleep in your bed."

"Why stop disrupting my life now that I've finally gotten a little used to it?" He leaned the pitchfork against the wall and crossed his iron-hard arms confidently over his broad chest "Besides, haven't I done a good job helping you out? I treated your wound. I made sure it was clean and bandaged. I saw that you and your family were safe and provided for."

"I don't know how I can ever repay you. No one person has ever done so much for me."

"And you thank me by leaving?"

I don't want to. Garnet felt her face flame from the edge of her dress's high collar to the roots of her hair. "Gus's cabin does have a wooden floor, so it will be considerably warmer in case we are forced to stay in town through the winter."

Wyatt snorted. "So, now you're comparing other men's cabin's to mine?"

"Then you tell me what to do, what other choice I can make. What if I can't earn enough money before the snow traps us here for months on end? If that happens, we can't all share your shack. It's unfair to you and it's inappropriate for two unmarried women to live with you."

"If you pay rent, then it will take you longer to earn enough money to head home." He took a step closer. "I know the real reason you want to leave."

"You do?" Perhaps it was the nearness of him that snatched her breath from her lungs.

"You can't keep secrets, Garnet. Not with that honest face of yours." A spot of humor sparkled in his wicked dark eyes, luminous and enchanting.

Her heart hammered far too fast. It was from fatigue, no doubt. Overwork. Certainly such palpitations were not due to his standing so close. She could see the individual whiskers darkening his strong jaw. "What secrets am I hiding?"

"Certain feelings. For me."

Did it show that much? "Perhaps just a few."

"It must hurt. Feeling obligated to a man in miner's garb, a man not so different from your pa."

"You think—" She thought he had guessed her feelings. That perhaps he felt the same way about her. But he didn't. Once again she was wrong due to her silly foolish heart.

A muscle jumped along his jaw. "There are two little words civilized women like you say all the time, but I haven't heard them pass your lips lately."

"Which words?"

"You know them." Wyatt stared harder at her mouth. "Come on. Say it."

"Say what?"

"You can thank me. Go on. It won't hurt you to say it. Much."

Oh, he could be charming when he wanted to be, with that lopsided grin and twinkle in his eyes. He watched her expectantly.

"Thank you." Why such a polite phrase stuck in her throat, she couldn't say. Nor could she explain the way she felt weak and invigorated at the same time. Or how daylight around them faded bit by bit until Wyatt was all she saw, all there was in the world. The warmth lighting his black eyes and an amused grin tugging up one corner of his mouth. Why, he even had attractive lips. She had never noticed it before. Not like this. Not so that her gaze centered on them and she could not look away.

"See? It didn't kill you to thank me."

"No, I guess it didn't. I'm still alive. My heart is still beating."

His smile broadened, and it was like the sun in the sky. "Everyone needs a little help now and then. Even you, Garnet."

"But do you? Do you need help?"

The brightness of his smile faded, like the sun setting behind clouds. He shook his head. "Not me. I never need anybody."

No, of course not. Garnet could feel her heart sink back down in her chest. Wyatt Tanner, so tough, so damnably male, certainly did not need someone like her.

And neither did she need him. Hadn't she learned through the years how disastrous it was to depend on a man? Depending on Wyatt for shelter through the winter might be a very bad mistake. She had watched her own mother die of a broken heart, yearning after a man who loved nobody more than himself.

But her logic failed as she gazed up into Wyatt's eyes. She saw strength, intelligence, and warmth. A softness had ebbed into his face like mist into the night, softening the chiseled angles of his cheekbones and the line of his carved chin.

He spoke, moving his mesmerizing lips, and she could not tear her gaze away. "I haven't needed anyone for as long as I've been on my own, nearly twenty years now. I was alone until you showed up. I had peace and quiet until all your admirers started bringing their rucksacks stuffed full of dirty clothes, trying to court you."

More than humor rang in his voice, a voice that enveloped her like a hug, that made her let down her guard and feel with her heart. This time, for the first time, there was something different, something frightening and dangerous in it.

The blood roared in her ears as she watched his mouth move over more words. He leaned closer, so close she could see nothing but the deep blackness of his eyes and the small chips of chocolate-brown within, warmer than hot coffee on a cold day. "There's something you should know."

"W-what?" Goodness, his lips were so close he was almost kissing her as he spoke. She could feel the heat from his mouth hover over her own.

"I've seen Gus's cabin. There's no well and there's no privy. It's also much smaller than mine."

"You don't think I should rent his cabin?"

Wyatt's upper lip brushed hers once. "No. It has a canvas roof and would be very drafty come winter."

"*Your* cabin has a canvas roof." How her mouth tingled with small fire-hot sparks.

"Not for long." His upper lip brushed hers again. Such sweetness. "Perhaps it would be better for you if you stay." Both his upper and bottom lips brushed hers as he spoke.

Tingling heat skidded across the sensitive skin of her mouth. Garnet had never felt anything so incredible in her entire life.

"Say yes," he whispered, right before nibbling her lips.

Exploding dynamite could not have surprised her more. She was all sensation, all aching want for his lips on hers, warm and tender and so brief he pulled away before she could even believe he had kissed her. Before her heart kicked and the fire in her veins ignited and she wanted nothing more than another kiss, but a longer one this time, one that would last forever and a day.

Something danced in those black eyes of his. Something like excitement and desire and downright amusement all mixed together in a heady brew. She knew, because that's how she felt.

What was happening to her? Her heart cracked a little bit. What was this powerful wildfire of excitement she felt for Wyatt? She had never experienced the like before. Was it infatuation? She was being foolish, wasn't she? Was she putting herself on the same path her mother had taken, allowing herself to give her affections to a man who loved no one more than a gamble? Wyatt was a miner dreaming of riches but living in complete squalor. He'd left a perfectly good job with the law to dig for gold. He was just as shiftless as Pa.

She gazed up into Wyatt's face. A strong man, but a man nonetheless. He could break her heart as easily as Pa had broken Ma's. How could she stay? How could she leave? And worse, was he just playing with her affections? She could not forget what Golda had said. Could not deny that Wyatt was lonely, too.

Garnet touched her lips. The tingling had faded but the memory of his kiss remained.

* * *

Wyatt couldn't sleep, so he wandered outside into the night. The stable was peaceable enough, just him and his horse, but he couldn't get a certain female out of his mind. The taste of her kiss, the warm velvet brush of her lips, the way she'd put her fingertips to her mouth afterward haunted him. No, tormented him. Because he wanted to do that again.

And that just went to show how daft he was. He was in this town for only one reason—to find his brother's killer. He didn't belong here, wouldn't stay here. What would happen then? One of his leads would pan out, he would arrest the murderer and head home, back to his job, back to his life. Garnet could be stuck here if the snows came early, with her own set of admirers and her cleaning business.

Her very successful cleaning business. At least four dozen shirts and trousers flapped on the makeshift clothesline in the breeze, with more heaped high inside the cabin, waiting to be washed. This influx of visitors was interfering with his investigation. He couldn't leave her unguarded to hunt down his leads.

Before this, his best information had often come from the taverns, over whiskey and poker and tongues made careless by alcohol. Instead of working tonight, he was here, sitting guard in the dark of night, troubled by a little tiny kiss he'd given a woman.

Not just any woman. No, Garnet was by far unlike any female he'd ever met. Porcelain-fine skin. A silken luxury of ebony hair. That spark of integrity in intelligent blue-green eyes. And a will the size of a mountain.

He heard the sound. The creaking of soft leather as the cabin door swung open. Turning, he waited, listening to her familiar shuffle. Her leg was almost fully healed, he realized with some satisfaction. She wasn't limping at all.

"Don't shoot," she teased. Light from a sickle moon glowed silver on her white wrapper. A small ruffle from her nightgown peeked out from underneath.

"You're in luck. I didn't even draw on you."

She moved with a regal grace. With the way the sheen of starlight cloaked her in silhouette, she looked like a fabled queen of old.

Wyatt shook his head. Apparently he had been drinking too much whiskey.

He recapped the bottle and set it aside. "I hope you know I'm missing out on my poker game tonight."

"Don't tell me you're a gambler, too." She halted with a small wobble before him. "Whiskey and cards." She sighed. "I guess that's a prospector's life."

"Not always. Not if there's better company to be had." Wyatt gestured to the dusty earth beside him. "I haven't always had a woman living with me before this. Come join me."

"I couldn't sleep either." A pleasant, light scent of roses filled the air as she settled on the ground beside him. "I miss home. I miss my house and my garden. And the harvest ... oh, I hope it went well. I left Ruby's husband in charge of the farm."

She scrubbed her face with her hands, clearly worried. Wyatt leaned his back against a large boulder. "What kind of farm?"

"We grow apples. Ma inherited the land from her family. Pa was never much of a provider, he was always drifting." She faced him, and only the faint ethereal light from the thin slivered moon separated each of them from the night. "What about you?"

"What about me?"

"Do you stay in one spot for the length of a season, or are you always moving on?"

He didn't like to talk about himself. First, it was the surest way to blow a cover. And besides, he never trusted anyone that much. His life was no one's business. And he opened his mouth intending to say so. "I was in the cavalry for ten years."

The words popped out of his mouth of their own volition, betraying how lonely he was, how drawn to this tender, steely-willed woman.

"The cavalry?"

"I got out years ago. I landed myself a job as a deputy in a few small towns and later as a sheriff in a fairly big town not far from here. I don't like to remember that time."

"Is that when you had that divorce?" She whispered the last word. Not with judgment, but with a need so raw in her voice, it frightened him.

"Yes." Wyatt felt his chest squeeze tight.

"Have you thought about settling down again?" So soft, those words.

"No." It was the truth, he realized. He had a fine enough home in Bannack, where he worked for the county judge, and a job he liked. But his heart, it was wandering, as restless and wild as the night wind. He doubted any woman could tame it, could make him trust in love and forever again. "Did I scare you tonight? I mean, after so many marriage proposals, my kiss might have been unwanted."

"Not unwanted."

Wyatt recognized something in her voice, a softening . . . of her, of him, of the distance between them. "I didn't mean—"

"Oh, I know." Too quickly, she interrupted him. "I have already forgotten it."

But her defenses had been knocked down and stayed down. Now Wyatt could see right through her, look right into her heart, lonely and wanting.

He felt the same way.

It would be so easy to say something humorous, to admit he

hadn't forgotten the sweet taste of her mouth and wasn't likely to. But where would that get him? Garnet didn't want him. She was as terrified of an involvement as he was. They were alike in that way. Besides, he didn't know what he wanted from her, except another kiss.

"Then what are we going to do about this?" he asked, gesturing between them. "What are we going to do about us? After all, I kissed you. Isn't that improper where you come from?"

"Absolutely, but these things happen."

"It was only a little kiss," he said.

"Hardly anything at all."

Wyatt brushed a finger along the edge of her soft face, tracing the line of her cheekbone. Her black hair curled in small wisps, dark silk against white satin. Her skin felt softer than anything he had ever known.

She didn't flinch, and he drew his finger away.

"Maybe we could be friends," he suggested now. He didn't know what else to say or do.

"Friends?" Garnet gazed up at him with her jeweled gaze. "In the whole of my life in Willow Hollow, I've never had a man extend me such an offer."

Wyatt saw her heart in her eyes, heard it in her words. "Must be a right unfriendly place you hail from."

"No," she smiled now, soft and captivating. "I just hadn't met you."

CHAPTER NINE

Garnet laid in bed and watched dawn color the canvas roof above her. First, the darkness waned, fading to a charcoal gray, then an almost lavender light. Soon, peach brushed the canvas, both the hue and light growing stronger until it glowed with pale orange sunshine. Birds in the trees began their happy songs, and Garnet felt happy, too. Happy, but troubled.

Oh, she'd tangled herself in a fine web. Agreeing to stay here in Wyatt's cabin while he'd kissed her. Even now, the luxury of that kiss, of his hot warm lips caressing hers, made the blood thrum in her veins. She was becoming infatuated with him, she had no doubt. It was very dangerous ground, and yet she could not seem to stop herself. Is this what happened to Ma? Had those first kisses led to more?

A cracking pain tore through her heart. She could not break the vow she'd made to herself, to never make the mistake her mother had. To never repeat her childhood by growing up to love a man who wouldn't stay, who wouldn't love her back.

But staying here didn't mean she would come to such an end. She had very practical reasons for being with Wyatt instead of accepting Gus's offer of a cabin. She did not know the man, for one. What sort of landlord would he be? Was he only a businessman looking for a renter, or did he expect something more from her?

Even now there was a crisp bite to the morning air. Soon it

would freeze and then, if the snows came early and heavy, they would be stranded here. The mountain passes would be far too treacherous for stagecoach travel.

Beside her, Golda made a delicate sigh in her sleep, a wistful sound as if she were having a pleasant dream.

Garnet had had one of those, too. It had involved Wyatt's deep voice rumbling in her ear. She'd sat so close to him she could feel the heat from his body through the cotton of her dress. His kiss had played a prominent role, the tingling feeling that started in her lips and then extended throughout her body.

Friends. That's what Wyatt had said. They were friends now. There would be no more kisses, which was a very good idea. Kisses could lead to all sorts of trouble. But a friend . . . why, that would be a good thing indeed. She wouldn't have to be alone, carrying her worries and troubles inside. She had Wyatt to talk to when she couldn't sleep, Wyatt who listened and who shared a part of his past with her.

She could have this remarkable friendship, as long as she kept her foolish heart under control. As long as her tingling body stopped aching for more of his kisses. Well, she was the epitome of self-control. Garnet Jones had willpower that could not be broken.

Friends. Yes, that was the perfect solution.

A ringing thud shattered the silence and she leaped out of bed. It sounded again as she burst out the door and squinted up into the morning light. "What are you doing?"

"Hammering a nail into this board." He grinned at her from his position on the ladder.

"It's not even six o'clock in the morning, far too early to be making that much racket."

"I'm putting an addition on my shack." Gentle morning sunshine outlined him, painting his muscular shape with light. His tan cotton shirt clung to his shoulders. His collar gaped open to reveal a glimpse of his throat and chest, and his rolled-up shirtsleeves showed the ripple of muscle in his forearms. My, he was such a well-built man, her pulse fluttered.

What was she doing? She had to stop thinking of him like that. He was her friend. Any feelings she had for him had to be of a strictly platonic nature.

"Are you sure you know what you're doing?" she asked now. It was her experience that prospectors didn't know a whole lot about work, carpentry or any other. Then she remembered Wyatt's story, how he'd been a deputy and a sheriff before he'd given up a life of responsibility.

"I have a hammer, don't I? I wouldn't have one if I didn't know how to use it."

"You *think* you know how to use it." She watched him fish for a nail in his shirt pocket and couldn't help but notice the strong chest beneath the shirt. "I happen to know a little something about carpentry."

"You?" He laughed. "I thought your specialty involved a washboard and lye soap."

"I'm a woman of many talents." She only then realized she was standing before him in her nightgown with her hair unbound and dancing in the wind. Goodness, this infatuation she had for Wyatt had to stop. She was losing all propriety and the last of her common sense. What scandalous thing would she do next? Well, in her present state of mind she might not even notice.

"I'll start breakfast," she offered, "while you play with your tools."

He tipped back his head to laugh, merriment in his eyes. "Fine. I have to take a quick trip to town this morning and then spend some time working my claim. I think you ought to be safe without me. There are so many men hanging around these days, dropping off or picking up their laundry."

"Ah yes, you want to go play in the creek." She'd almost forgotten that Wyatt was a wanderer and a gambler, just as Pa was. A man who searched for treasure. "I'll let you know when the eggs are ready."

"There's someone coming." He stood on the sloping rafter, straining to see. "Yep. If I don't miss my guess, that looks like Gus's bay gelding."

"Gus?" She was not dressed for company or for turning down a perfectly good rental house. This only proved it. She'd completely lost her mind.

* * *

"You mean we're staying?" Golda tossed down her hairbrush. "I heard what Gus offered you. If we lived in town, we'd be closer to Lance."

"Yet another reason to stay here." Garnet rolled her eyes. She was happy for the first time in her life, and she wasn't going to let her sister, still unhappy over her separation from Lance, ruin it. "Wyatt will not charge us rent, unlike Gus Adams. We will be able to save our money faster and leave this town much sooner."

Well, leaving had seemed like a good idea. That was before she'd found a friend in Wyatt.

"I can't believe this." Golda clenched her soft hands tight in her lap. Her mouth pursed in clear disapproval. "After all your lectures, you want to stay in this awful cabin because of him."

"Of Wyatt?" Was it that obvious? Could anyone look at her and know how she felt about the man? "I told you, staying here is the most logical choice."

"I see how you look at Mr. Tanner. All these years I've endured your warnings on falling in love with men just like him, and look at you. You're doing the very thing you lecture against. Are you that desperate?"

"I am a woman, too. All those years of responsibility were hard, and I got stuck with it because Ma was so ill and there was no one else. I never asked for something for myself because one of my younger sisters always needed something more, and I never complained. Not once. Until now. I want this, Golda. I want to stay here. We will be leaving for home soon enough. I expect you not to say another word against me."

"I'll make sure she doesn't," Wyatt said from the doorway, his voice low and dangerous.

Garnet spun around. Shock and embarrassment tightened her throat. She couldn't force out the words of denial and apology. Did Wyatt think she was sweet on him? Is that why he'd dared to kiss her? Had he thought she was so desperate she would easily give him her affections?

She had been a fool indeed. A fool to think she could somehow have a friend in a man, even one as wonderful as Wyatt. Didn't she deserve something all her own, just this once? Something that didn't involve working to provide for others? She would be leaving in a few weeks by her calculations, as long as the snows held off, and in the meantime didn't she deserve a friend? Couldn't she just enjoy a little human contact?

Not now, now that he knew how lonely she was, how vulnerable her heart.

She feared Wyatt was no better than her Pa had been, a wanderer, a man who used a woman's affections to his own advantage. After all, why would a man show interest in a woman as plain and prickly as her?

With a heavy heart, she reached for the frying pan.

* * *

Watching Garnet practically throw herself at that Mr. Tanner was about to make Golda ill. How many years did she have to listen to her clench-jawed, stern-eyed older sister extol the virtues of independent females?

All of her life, that's how long. For fifteen years she'd had to endure Garnet's lectures on men, on the pleasure men wanted from a girl, of how terribly men treated women. And for what?

To watch Garnet fill up a less-than-civilized man's battered old tin coffee cup.

Oh, there was no eyelash-batting and no coy little bobs of the head. Mr. Tanner wasn't the kind of man drawn to those types of affectations in a woman. He actually seemed to like Garnet's stern-faced approach to life. Seated across from each other at the small, miserable excuse for a table, they were discussing carpentry methods and how best to put a roof and an addition on this sorry excuse for a shack.

Mr. Tanner wanted to build large enough rooms for all of them to winter comfortably here, should the need arise.

Golda shook her head in silent disapproval. As she poked the egg on her new plate with the fork Garnet had bought at that tolerable little store in town, Golda watched the yellow yolk run into her thin slab of salt pork. A deep resentment began to build in her belly so that she wasn't hungry at all.

All those years of lecturing and warnings, and look how Garnet was setting herself up for the very folly she preached against. Anyone could see the type of cloth Mr. Tanner was cut from, and was her older sister as desperate as all that? There was no mistaking the gleam of interest in Garnet's eyes.

And surly Mr. Tanner was nearly friendly with each response. There was, of course, only one thing a man like him would want from a woman, and Tanner wasn't one to offer a wedding ring. Not like her dear, sweet, noble Lance. Even now, excitement fluttered through her.

He would be here soon, with a ring, with a horse, and with real promises he meant to keep. He was honest and respectable, come to find his fortune in this harsh country. He would make something of himself, whereas Mr. Tanner would always remain . . . despicable.

It was all Golda could do to hide her sneer. She might have lived a sheltered life in Willow Hollow, but she had observed Ruby's husband over the past year of their marriage. He didn't seem to bring down the kind of catastrophe on Ruby that Garnet was always warning against.

And when Ruby's life hadn't turned miserable, when she hadn't come running home from abuse or neglect or hardship, Garnet had simply dismissed the husband as being one of those rare men who were not so deeply disagreeable as to beat their wives or require constant supervision.

Well, Garnet might think she knew everything, but Golda had seen quite a bit of the world now and felt confident in her own decision-making. Not all men were as bad as she had been led to believe. There might be those like Mr. Tanner and those frightening men in town, but there had been kind Elmer and generous Gus and that pleasant store owner. Lance was among those sort, a man she could give her life to.

Golda sliced off a bit of egg with her fork. She had to eat, despite the disgust at her sister's antics and the excitement shivering in her belly. Today would be the longest—and the best—day of her life.

* * *

Having Garnet in his life was seriously compromising his investigation. Wyatt pulled the leather drawstring poke from his pocket and fished inside it for a small nugget.

"I will have my hired boy load the lumber you purchased into your wagon." Barrett Carson hauled out his gold scale and took a careful step. "Did Miss Garnet accompany you to town this morning?"

"No, she's home scrubbing clothes." Wyatt tossed the nugget on the polished counter and studied the man before him carefully. "Every unmarried man in this town has shown up on my doorstep with their laundry in hand. She'll have the entire population of Stinking Creek shining clean in no time."

"She's a woman of fortitude."

Wyatt didn't like Carson's tone. Didn't like the gleam of interest in his beady little eyes. "She is leaving town in a few weeks if the weather holds. She is not looking for marriage."

"A woman can always be tempted."

Wyatt resisted the urge to punch the smug grin off the shopkeeper's mouth. He knew beyond a doubt Garnet could not be tempted. She didn't care about a man's money. She was more than happy to stay with him, more than willing to share a kiss and friendship beneath a moonlit sky. She wasn't going to run off on a man to enjoy the company of another who could give her more in the way of material possessions. Garnet was loyal and honest, he'd learned this by watching her.

And she was his.

He had vowed never to become involved with another woman again. Only a woman could break his heart the way Amelia had. Only a woman could hold all of a man's fragile trust, love, and hope in her hand. And when they were broken, how could they ever be repaired?

Now he knew. He'd been lonely for so long. Lonely by choice, because he never met one woman who could be what he needed. Until now. Until Garnet.

He grabbed his box of supplies. Maybe it wasn't such a bad thing, deciding to try again. Then again, maybe it was. Garnet had a life and a home. And he had an investigation and a job waiting for him far from here.

"That's quite a nugget, Tanner. You must have a good claim."

"Won it in a poker game." Wyatt considered Barrett Carson again. He was a wealthy man's youngest son, proving his worth to his father by working in this store. Educated, articulate, and high society, Wyatt figured. He'd learned at his late-night poker games that Carson was unhappy working for his father, didn't like Stinking Creek, wanted out of Montana.

"You win all your gold in poker games," Carson observed, but didn't take a step. As if he were hiding a possible limp.

"I win it the easy way. Why does it matter to you where I get my gold?"

"No reason." Carson's hat could hide a bandage.

Wyatt wasn't fooled. Whoever killed his brother had known Ben had panned a lot of gold, for robbery had been the real reason behind the murder. He'd started his footwork in the same saloons where his brother had spent lonely nights playing cards. And betting those fifty-dollar nuggets. It was the primary place Ben had spent his gold.

Now, looking at the panning supplies in the corner of the store, and then at the guns behind glass against the back wall, Wyatt had to move Carson up on his list of suspects. "You carry a good selection."

Carson grabbed his key to the case. "Are you looking for a new rifle?"

"I found one just like this on the road one night. Wondered how much it was worth."

Carson bowed his head. He fumbled with the key-chain. "You wouldn't get as much second-hand."

"Probably not." Wyatt wondered about the shopkeep. "Is this the only place in town that sells guns like these?"

"Well, there's the gunsmith down the street."

"Right. I'd forgotten." Wyatt hadn't forgotten. He knew how much a rifle was worth. "Sell many of these?" He pointed at a gleaming Winchester.

"None in at least a month."

"Is that right? Figured the man who lost the rifle might have replaced it."

"Not from this store."

"I appreciate your time, Carson." Wyatt headed toward the door, his instincts unsettled.

"Do you want your change in gold or coin?" the merchant asked, stepping behind the safety of the counter.

"Credit. Put it on Garnet's account."

"Whatever you say. With all the lonely men in town, is Miss Garnet getting a lot of suitors?"

Wyatt considered that question, too. "Yes, Carson. She sure is."

"Do you know what kind of candy she likes?"

"Expensive." Wyatt turned to the door. With any luck Garnet would hate whatever candy Carson brought. He headed down the street to pay a visit to the gunsmith.

* * *

Garnet picked her way along the trail that followed the muddy banks of Stinking Creek. A rabbit darted out of the low bushes and across the path. A puff of cold wind rattled the alders overhead. Birds scurried about their work, and the crackling expectation in the air signaled a storm was coming.

There he was, just up ahead. Her heart gave a jump at the sight of him. Wyatt knelt at the creek's bank, his hat tipped over his eyes, his wide shoulders braced as he shook a broad shallow pan.

"You shouldn't sneak up on an armed man." He didn't look up as he worked.

She picked her way across the uneven ground. "I didn't know you were armed."

"Aside from the intruder you wounded, now and then someone decides it's easier to steal the gold than it is to work for it."

"I didn't know panning for gold was work."

"Well, maybe it's time you learned." Humor flashed in his eyes. "Come sit down by me."

"No, I have laundry hanging on the line that needs ironing and—"

"Sit down." Firmer this time, brooking no argument. He held out his big hand, wet and muddy.

Her foolish feet carried her forward. She placed her hand in his. "Do you actually find any gold?"

"Sometimes." Wyatt tugged her down to kneel beside his big steely body.

She felt his heat, his strong hard presence in tune with the wilderness surrounding them. His voice rumbled through her as if it were her own.

"What amazes me is the earth." How reverent he sounded. "Something of great value is hidden beneath all this dirt and rock. Plain ordinary dirt. You can't tell where it is by looking. But a patient man can brush away the ordinary, bit by bit, and find the treasure beneath."

"You make it sound almost noble, but I'm not fooled." But she was captivated by this man wearing plain, ordinary clothes, living a plain, ordinary life.

"Here. Put your hand on this." His fingers wrapped around hers and set them on the edge of his pan. The metal was wet from the creek water and warm from his touch. "And your other hand here."

"You're trying to convert me into being a prospector."

"I'm trying to prove you wrong." His eyes sparkled with amusement and warmth and caring. "Now, shake it like this, back and forth."

"It's like flouring a cake pan."

He laughed. "Watch. See how the water is moving the dirt. Look, right there. You've found gold."

"This is your gold."

"Isn't it fun?"

"You're not going to get me to change my opinion." But she laughed, in spite of herself. The dull glint of gold amid the tiny rocks and bits of earth was fascinating. "All right, I admit it. It's fun."

"Keep going. Look at that. You've panned yourself a good-sized nugget."

She stilled the pan while he reached for the dull, muddy gold rock. "That couldn't be worth much."

"About fifty dollars is my guess." His smile broadened and etched dimples into his cheeks, dimples she'd never seen before.

She knew so little about him, only that he was everything she should never want in a man, and she wanted him. How she wanted him.

"Fifty dollars?"

"It's yours. That will buy your stage passage to the Montana border."

"Only one ticket."

"Maybe you could sell that sister of yours."

She felt lighter than she'd ever been before. "I pity the poor man who would pay good money for her. She doesn't cook so well."

"Don't talk about leaving. This place isn't going to be the same when you go. It will be pretty quiet around here without your humming and chatter."

"You would miss me?"

"Sure." His gaze roamed across her face. Then he took the gold nugget and bent to rinse it in the creek water. "Without all those suitors and clients coming around to call on you, I'm going to be mighty lonely."

"So it's the visitors and not me you'll miss."

"That's right."

This time she could tell for certain he was only teasing her, saying words that were not true to hide the things that were. Did he care for her? Did he feel as she did, confused but attracted?

All the more reason to resist her physical desire for him. They were friends, nothing more. They could never be anything more. She could never trust a man that much, not enough to hand over her heart.

He dried the nugget on his shirtfront, then pressed it into her hand. The metal held his heat, special to her because he had touched it. "Want to pan for more?"

She swallowed. If she found more gold, then she would have more money to go home with. She would have to leave sooner, maybe as soon as tomorrow, when the stage was due. Maybe she could find enough to see her home in time to start her term of teaching. She would be back where she belonged, where she was safe.

Her heart sank. Maybe that wasn't what she wanted now, after all. She'd sort of gotten used to the idea of staying in Montana for a little while and experiencing some of the things that she'd never had the chance to do before she returned home.

Thunder crashed overhead, a deafening crack that seemed to rend the world in two. Wyatt jumped up, cursing. Lightning tore across the sky, streaking toward the earth. Fire lit up the forest not ten yards from them. The earth shook, wood splintered, and a treetop, struck by the dangerous lightning bolt, tumbled to the ground, flames and smoke rising.

"Stay right there," Wyatt ordered. "Keep away from the trees."

"Where are you going?"

Any moment that lightning could return, closer this time. It could strike him, but did that stop Wyatt? No, he had a bucket of water in hand. He began dousing the flaming branches, trying to stop the spread of fire to the tinder-dry grasses.

Well, she wasn't going to stand around like this. She slipped the nugget into her skirt pocket for safekeeping and submerged the gold pan into the creek. Water dripping, she hurried to the flames and put out an ignited limb all on her own.

"Get down," he shouted above the thunder.

"The faster this fire is out, the faster we can both be safe."

He growled, racing the few feet to the river. Of course he wouldn't see it that way. He probably thought he could save the day while she sat around complimenting him for it. She filled her pan and after a few trips, the flames were out and the lightning strikes were moving southward across the creek.

"You're a crazy woman, do you know that?"

She laughed, breathless. Was it from running? Or from watching the broad span of his chest rise and fall with each breath? "I guess it depends on whether or not you like crazy women."

"Then I'm in luck." He held out his hand, reaching for hers.

Pleasant tingles danced from her fingers all the way up her arm. The contact of his skin against hers reminded her of their differences. He was rough and callused, hard and powerful, but flesh and bone, just as she was.

Something cold struck her face. "No, it can't be."

"It's just rain. It won't hurt you."

"No, but it could ruin the clothes I left out on the line. Hurry!" She started off at a run and raced along the narrow path.

"Rain can't hurt a pair of trousers." Wyatt kept up with her, one step behind.

"Yes, but I'll have to rewash them and lose all of today's hard work." Her foot slid on a patch of mud. Wyatt's hand cupped her elbow, catching her. Together they broke out of the forest and dashed across the yard.

The huge raindrops had already soaked them and turned the inches-thick dust to mud.

"You run pretty fast for a woman," he taunted as he passed her.

"You're kind of slow for a man." She made him laugh and by the time she turned the corner of the cabin, just three paces behind, he was already tugging shirts and trousers off the line. She joined him and in no time at all they had the garments laid out in the fresh dry straw in the stable. Perhaps they could be salvaged.

"You know what I could use?"

The lure in his voice made her think he might want to kiss her again. Rain dripped off his hat brim and plastered his cotton shirt to his chest like a second skin. She saw every delineated, well-defined muscle, every curve and plane and dip.

Her throat constricted. Every part of her ached to lay her hand there, on his breastbone, over his rapidly beating heart.

"I'm afraid to ask," she confessed.

His chuckle brushed over her like rain. "I noticed we ran out of coffee beans. I picked up another pound at Carson's store."

"Wyatt, that would make you the hero of my dreams."

"Gee, if I had known that, I would have got the more expensive beans."

The mare whinnied in her stall, lifting her nose high to scent the wind.

"Someone's coming." Wyatt took her arm and moved past her. "Wait. I can see him from here. It's Carson.

And it looks like he's carrying a box of candy. Do you like

candy better than coffee beans?"

"No, why?" And she didn't like Barrett Carson.

"Then I'm in luck. Come on, go send that dandy home and I'll brew you a cup of real coffee, Montana style."

"Is that a promise or a threat?"

His gaze flickered with mystery. "You'll have to live dangerously and find out."

* * *

Wyatt watched while Garnet tried her first sip of his best coffee. "What do you think?"

"This tastes like mud." Her lush mouth twisted. "Bitter mud. You wouldn't happen to have any sugar around here, would you?"

"Nope. I didn't think of it." And he should have. He should have guessed a woman like Garnet, particular in every way, would drink her coffee sweetened.

"I'll just have to improvise. Look, we'll use Mr. Carson's chocolates." Pleased with herself, Garnet leaned back in the chair to reach the decorated box with the tips of her fingers. She tore the wrapping open and plopped one of the fine chocolates into her brand new tin cup. "Now, I'll just wait for this to melt, stir it around, and then I'll see if I can stomach your coffee."

Wyatt could see the happiness gleam like a precious gem in her eyes, in those blue eyes the color of a mountain lake. Unusual eyes for an unusual woman. "Give me one of those chocolates."

"What? A tough loner like you has a sweet tooth?"

"You have no idea." Wyatt reached for a piece of candy, figuring Carson would be none too happy to know Garnet wasn't the only one enjoying those chocolates. He plopped it in his cup and watched Garnet laugh.

She had changed into a different dress after their dash in the rain, a soft white garment flecked with hundreds of tiny green leaves. White buttons marched from her chin to her waist, accenting a softly shaped bodice and firm breasts.

The skirt was plain, without a bustle or hoops, but it was elegant. The white and leaf-green sprigged material made her look fresh, like the world after a spring rain. Her raven hair was tied back with a white length of muslin, and small wisps had escaped to frame her face. Wyatt stared at the contrast, the white dress and black hair, the soft leaf imprinted on fabric and the porcelain clearness of her face.

Want, long denied, burned in his chest. The memory of kissing her teased him. As she lifted her sparkling tin cup and delicately sipped from the rim as if it were the finest of china, her merry gaze met his.

"The chocolate makes this mud you made quite tolerable. Try it." Steadfast and loyal, honest and passionate. Garnet licked her lush lips with the pink tip of her tongue and set his blood on fire.

With a bright flash of clarity Wyatt knew he liked this woman far more than was prudent. He couldn't help himself. He leaned across the corner of the table and cupped the back of her head, her satiny hair luxurious against his fingers, and brought her mouth to his.

She tasted of coffee and chocolate and a sweet fire all her own. Every inch of his body strummed with desire for her, only her. He laved his tongue along her lower lip. And when she opened her mouth to him, so willing and eager, he forgot every reason why he shouldn't become involved with her. He explored the even row of her front teeth, took courage from the low moan in her throat. She liked this, too, this intimacy.

Then a knock pounded on the door. Garnet skidded away from him, her hand to her mouth. Rain dripped from the corner of the roof, where it was collecting on the canvas cover. Who would be visiting in a storm?

"Golda. She's back from town." Garnet stood so fast, she knocked over the chair. The impact of Wyatt's kiss burned along her lips. She couldn't look at him as she pulled the latch and tugged open the door.

"Ma'am?"

It wasn't Golda, but a skinny boy in a big slicker, rain dripping off his floppy-brimmed hat. He was muddy from head to toe.

"Are you inquiring about my cleaning services?"

"No—uh," the boy hesitated, rolling his eyes to the sky as if looking for the right words. "Some woman paid me to deliver this. Let me find it."

Garnet watched while the lad opened his slicker and searched both trouser pockets. Finally he held out a folded sheet of paper. She could only stare at it. "What's this?"

"Don't know." The young man turned and ran back out into the rain.

Garnet felt the telltale pitter in her heart that foretold disaster. She unfolded the scrap of paper, her fingers trembling. She recognized Golda's fancy, precise handwriting.

Dearest Sister,

Please find it in your heart to be glad for me, your baby sister. Lance asked me to be his wife. We are running off to Virginia City to be wed.

CHAPTER TEN

"What's wrong?" Wyatt's steps sloshed in the mud behind her. "Couldn't Toby afford your laundry service?"

Garnet's hand began to tremble. She could not believe this letter, that this was real, that Golda would show such a lack of good sense and run off with a man who didn't even own his tent outright.

"Garnet." His hands cupped her shoulders from behind, such big, comforting hands. How she wanted to lean against him and ask for his help. How wonderful it would be to depend on him, to place her trust in him.

But how could she? Golda wasn't his problem. And he was a friend, nothing more. The way he'd kissed her so intimately . . . why, she blushed thinking of how his tongue had caressed hers and made her body melt.

How could she rely on a man she wanted to seduce her?

"Bad news?"

Garnet crumpled the paper into a tight ball. "No, of course not. I was just surprised, that's all."

"Surprised? You look ready to cry."

"I am just a bit distressed, but nothing for you to worry about."

"Nothing?" He spun her around so only a tiny breath stood between them.

Garnet gazed up into his eyes and saw an affection so big and bright she could almost believe it. Could it be true? Could he care about her, too? Something in her heart flared again, like a small bit of paper catching a spark. "It's a personal note."

"Not from Barrett Carson, I hope." Black brows rose in a skeptical line. "I think he wants you. That was an expensive box of candy."

"I don't know what Mr. Carson thinks he sees in me." She shrugged, far too troubled over what to do and torn over asking Wyatt for help.

His hand curled over hers. "He sees a beautiful woman full of principles and convictions."

"Principles? Convictions?" She almost snorted.

"That's the woman I see, too. There was such tenderness in his voice, and it rumbled through her with the power of thunder.

Did he truly think so? Garnet could only try to measure the sincerity in his eyes.

What kind of principles did she have, enjoying kisses from a man who knew no permanence in his life? Or living in his cabin without the sanctity of marriage? Back home in Willow Hollow that would make her quite an indecent woman. Decent people would cross the street to avoid her.

"Let me see." He took the paper from her grip, simply, easily, and unballed it.

Her heart thudded in her chest. Wyatt had righted the page and was squinting at it, studying the words intently. "Your sister and her admirer are marrying just for a roll in the sheets?"

"Wyatt! That's my sister you are talking about. She is an innocent, do you understand me? She does not roll in the sheets with anyone, particularly any prospector."

"And what is that supposed to mean?" Wyatt crumpled the paper in one fist, his broad shoulders set, his powerful gaze riveted on hers. He made her feel small and foolish and . . . oh, how did she explain?

"I'm a prospector. Do you mean I am not good enough for you?" His anger came quietly.

You are more than good enough, her heart answered. But then her mind argued, *You are too much like Pa.* But it wasn't true. Wyatt did work his claim hard, he had an admirable work ethic for a prospector, and he was the only man she'd ever wanted to kiss. The only man she ever wanted to hold in her arms and never let go, to stay with, to feel his touch, know everything inside his heart.

Embarrassed, she lowered her gaze. "I was speaking about Lance, not you. Never you."

His thumb nudged her chin upward. A fading hurt reflected in his eyes. She'd hurt his feelings. Her chest tightened and she bit her lip, furious at herself for speaking without thinking.

"Surely your sister is of a marriageable age. I know you raised her, Garnet. I know you feel a great responsibility to see to her welfare. Just tell me what's bothering you. Tell me what's wrong with Lance."

She blinked hard so that the tears forming in her eyes wouldn't fall and show her for the weak, softhearted fool she was. "Lance is a drifter, a *dreamer*, a ne'er-do-well."

"A man like your pa?"

She nodded. "I can't think of a worse fate." The very idea of Golda wanting that dreamer was more than she could bear. "You don't understand. Pa got to do whatever he wanted, but not me. I had to stay and worry whether or not the crop would fail and we would have nothing but turnips to eat through the winter. I had to worry about the mortgage and the harvesting and finding enough money for doctor bills. I don't want that life for my sister, don't you understand?"

A choked sob resonated in the night. Rain dripped from the tear in the roof and plopped in the growing puddle on the floor between them.

"You're free from all that responsibility and worry, Garnet. Can't you see that?" His voice was a gruff, low rumble and so caring it was nothing short of magic. "You can do anything you want from this point on."

Garnet feared she might have imagined his empathy, but his work-roughened finger brushed against her cheek, wiping off the salty tears that stung her face. He was right, she knew it. She wasn't on the farm, Golda had run off, her responsibilities were over. Almost.

"Don't push me away," he asked now, an affection lighting his eyes. "I thought we agreed to be friends. Good friends. I've told you things about me I have never told any woman."

Garnet saw the raw power of this man's heart. Sincere and loyal and so tender she'd never seen the like. A deep yearning filled her chest. All she wanted was him. She wanted him more than anything she'd ever known.

She could no longer deny her strong feelings, this weakness for Wyatt Tanner. She firmed her chin against the most painful truth: She could not do everything alone. And she no longer wanted to. "I need your help, Wyatt. I need you."

His eyes darkened and he leaned close until their lips met in a dance of heat and warm velvet. She closed her eyes, wrapped her arms around his neck, and let herself feel what it was like to be good and truly kissed.

* * *

"W hat do ya keep lookin' back fer?" Lance asked in Golda's ear, his arms comfortable around her as they rode together over the trail toward Virginia City and matrimony.

If only they were headed there on a fine stepping horse instead of a borrowed donkey, but Golda knew she couldn't be particular. Not until Lance struck it rich on his claim. Then only the best-blooded stallions would pull their luxury carriage.

"I have this prickly feeling on the back of my neck." She didn't see anyone on the muddy trail behind them. Thunder cracked, and the donkey gave an awful, ear-splitting bellow. "I get this feeling every time Garnet is watching me do something she doesn't approve of."

"It's jest yer imagination." Lance squeezed her in a warm, wonderful hug.

Oh, with his big strong body warm against hers, she couldn't wait to become his wife. Her entire person was aflame with all sorts of desires.

If Garnet lacked the good sense to leave her alone and showed up to do anything to stop her wedding, Golda wouldn't stand for it. She loved Lance. She didn't need her big bossy sister ruining her happiness anymore. She was a grown woman, old enough to be a wife. And no jealous old spinster was going to destroy her chance to marry a man who was going to be rich one day.

* * *

G arnet tried to concentrate on her packing. Rain kept leaking from the roof and the afternoon was ebbing away. Wyatt had raced to town to secure the necessary items they would need for their trip to Virginia City.

She folded her nightgown, a serviceable white flannel garment, and stuffed it into her cracked valise. She was tormented by their brief kiss. All sliding tongues and lips and desire. That kiss was far too intimate; she did not believe it proper in the slightest for a man to kiss a woman unless they were engaged. But she hadn't cared one whit for her principles while enfolded in Wyatt's arms, opening her mouth to his.

It didn't matter how sensible she was, she wanted to feel passion. She'd never understood that yearning until now, until Wyatt had made her feel protected and special. Until he had kissed her lips and held her tight against his strong chest, and she had felt dizzy with that closeness, with wanting more than a kiss.

Heavens, she was slipping. Actually allowing herself to fall victim to a man's charm. Worse, she was liking it.

* * *

Wyatt ambled over to the bar, tugged out a stool, and sat on it. "Bring me a bottle," he instructed the barkeep when the elderly man limped over.

"That Miss Garnet shore is nice." The bartender grinned kindly as he set an unopened bottle and a clean shot glass on the polished bar between them. "She done agreed to clean up for me once a week and it's my pleasure to have her do it. It's mighty nice to have a proper woman in these parts, ain't it?"

Wyatt stared helplessly at the opened bottle, feeling the fresh jab of pain in his heart. "She's proper, all right." Her very improper, uninhibited kiss still scorched like fire across the surface of his lips.

The barkeep leaned both elbows on the counter. "Look around. Look what she done. Nearly every man in this town is shaved and showered. I heard Carson's store ran clean outta soap. I've been thinkin' of gussyin' myself up ever since I heard she's unmarried. I shore would like to have her for a wife. Is she pretty. Wow-ee."

Wyatt slammed the shot glass down on the counter. Jealousy thundered through his chest. Jealousy? Of course not! He wasn't jealous.

Yet as he poured his own whiskey, watching the sweet clear liquid splash into the chunky glass, unbidden thoughts flashed through his mind. Garnet with the long fall of raven-black hair cascading down her back, caressed lovingly by the wind. Garnet standing in the sunlight in that white dress sprinkled with small green leaves, so fresh . . . like a vision of the home he had always drawn in his mind. Garnet clinging to his arms, trembling with passion as he'd kissed her. He drained the shot glass and still he could remember holding her tight to his chest. She was all inviting curves and tempting woman.

And there was more. He could remember the taste of her mouth, velvet-warm and uncertain, soft as the morning. He could imagine what it might be like to kiss her more intimately, to unfasten those prim buttons marching down the front of her bodice and touch her lily-white skin.

Wyatt choked on the next image imprinted in his brain. He sputtered whiskey, coughed, but still the picture remained in his mind, all hot passion and fantasy. Garnet naked and reaching out her arms to welcome him.

Wyatt closed his eyes, leaned his elbow on the edge of the bar and buried his face in his hand. If he were more of a religious man, he'd ask the good Lord to help him, to save him from his own base desires. But Wyatt knew enough about himself, and about sex and desire, to know he wasn't lusting after Garnet.

He was in love with her.

* * *

Garnet was in a hurry, but she didn't wish to be rude. Sweet Katy, a kindly looking woman from one of the brothels, had stopped her on the street to inquire about laundry services. She couldn't turn away business, but then she realized Sweet Katy was inquiring about a job. Katy was thinking of finding something respectable, and Garnet could not turn her down. The woman was trying to improve her life, after all.

Sweet Katy mentioned that with the miners gussying themselves up and wearing clean clothes, she'd noticed some of the men were quite handsome. She'd always hoped to be a proper wife and mother one day, for she'd had little choice in her profession a few years ago. So Garnet promised Katy a job upon her return from Virginia City.

Outside the Stinking Creek Saloon, Garnet squared her shoulders. She had never been inside such an establishment before. But this was Montana Territory, not Willow Hollow, New York, and she was no longer the same woman she'd been when she first stepped foot off that stagecoach.

She recognized him at once among the din and the crush of men drinking booze. She would recognize Wyatt anywhere, even from behind. Those shoulders, strong enough to best any man in a fight. The powerful way he leaned forward on the bar stool, all steely confidence.

"Whiskey is *not* a necessary supply for our trip." She reached for the bottle.

Wyatt scooted it away.

"You broke the last one you touched," he explained with a grimace. "Besides, I'll need whiskey if you insist on making the coffee."

"Well, if you make the coffee I'll need to take Mr. Carson's chocolates."

"You will do no such thing." Stony anger distorted his face.

Was he jealous? No, he couldn't be. That didn't make sense. He was the one who suggested they should be friends. Then again, he was the one who had initiated all three of their kisses, especially the last, where he'd kissed her so deeply and boldly every inch of her body had craved more. And still craved it.

Intrigued, she sat down on the vacant stool beside him. The barkeep wandered over, a kindly, worn-out looking man carrying a fresh jug of whiskey, but she shook her head to decline his silent offer. She may be a new woman, but she wasn't about to sample spirits.

"Miss Garnet," a man's smooth-as-silk voice purred from behind.

She twisted to face him. She recognized his handsome face at once, polished in the way of money and social standing, but not attractive the way Wyatt was. "Hello, Mr. Carson. Thank you again for the gift of chocolates."

He removed his hat with a flourish. "I am deeply gratified to do anything I can for a fine woman like you."

Wyatt's hand closed over hers, commanding and possessive. "We'd better leave now. I see Tom outside with the horses. Let's go. Say good-bye, Carson."

Why, he truly was jealous! Garnet bit her lip so she wouldn't laugh. She bid Mr. Carson a hasty good-bye as Wyatt nearly pulled her out onto the street.

"Wyatt, not so fast."

"We need to hurry."

"Of course. Lance and Golda have several hours of a head start on us."

"I was thinking more of getting you away from Carson." He

released his hold on her wrist. "Don't worry. I'll find your sister. Count on me."

"I will." Something in her heart let go, something she'd been holding on to for so long—her inability to trust. But she could trust Wyatt. She would wager she could trust him with her life.

"Do you know how to ride?" he asked, great doubt booming low in his voice.

"Probably better than you." She turned to study the three horses at the hitching post. Wyatt's black mare, a sturdy packhorse loaded with supplies and sparse baggage, and a docile sorrel gelding that looked at her with big moon eyes. "Where's the sidesaddle?"

"A sidesaddle?" Wyatt tipped back his head, laughing. "I doubt there is one in the whole of Montana Territory."

"Well, how do civilized women ride?"

"Like men. Astride."

"Why—" That didn't sound decent at all.

* * *

Garnet could smell Virginia City before she saw it. A mix of odors that ranged from garbage to wood smoke to the scents of baking breads and smokehouses.

The city was nothing more than a grim stretch of buildings crammed along the wrinkled hillside. Yet in the night, with the slightest crescent of a moon, the entire town shone with an eerie candor. She had stayed a few days in Virginia City before catching the stage to Stinking Creek. She hadn't liked it.

Now, she had to find her sister. At the worst, Golda and Lance were only an hour or so ahead of them. Surely they could catch them in time. There was hope.

"Perhaps it's too late at night to find a minister to marry them." She leaned back in the saddle, attempting to post but failing as the horse trotted down the side of the hill. Her pantalooned bottom slapped against the hard saddle with every jarring step, and it hurt. Very much.

Beside her, seated on his proud horse, Wyatt shrugged. She could see the silhouette of his form, of man and horse, elegant and strong and bracing. He cleared his throat. "Don't count on it. You can buy anything anytime in this town, even a minister. You only need the money."

"Lance is pretty poor. Maybe they will have to wait until morning."

"He hasn't been very lucky on his claim."

"How do you know?"

"Oh, I have my ways." He tipped back his hat to stare at the town. "I used to spend my evenings in the saloon until a certain woman stumbled into my life. I pay attention, and it doesn't take long to figure out who has a good claim and who doesn't."

"Because they have the gold to gamble?"

"Exactly." His face compressed with thought, showing an intelligence she knew was there all along.

"Let me guess. You are not one of the men who spends his gold freely."

"Not until today. I had to buy those two horses and our supplies." He held out his hand. "Look. The rain is turning to snow."

"I see." The snow was significant because it meant she might be trapped in Stinking Creek for the winter. With Wyatt. With her growing desire for him, a desire she feared she could not resist.

Best to concentrate on the task ahead and not on the man riding at her side. "Do you know where we should start searching? I don't see any churches."

"I know Virginia City like the back of my hand." Mischief sparkled in his eyes. "Trust me. It won't be too hard to find all the ministers in this town."

How wonderful to have his help, Garnet marveled. She could get used to having such a strong shoulder to lean on. "You don't think they're married yet, do you?"

"Could be." He sounded noncommittal.

"She better not be." She didn't want Golda—or herself—to make a life-altering mistake.

Wyatt took the lead on the narrowing path, the mud making a sucking sound as the horses trotted. A crisp breeze blew down from the mountains and fat flakes whispered to the ground. Snow collected on the brim of her bonnet and she shook it off.

"Are you cold?" Wyatt twisted around in his saddle.

"I'm perfectly fine," she lied. Her bottom felt so sore from contact with the unyielding leather saddle it hardly mattered if she was soaked through to the skin.

"Does your behind hurt?"

"Something fierce."

"You don't have much further to ride. We're almost there."

"Those were the longest ten miles of my life."

His chuckle warmed her clear through, chasing away the chill in her bones and all her discomfort. "After you've found your sister, we'll get you in a hot bath and you can soak those saddle pains away."

"Oh, don't tease me. I want one right now!"

The sky chose that moment to send down great sheets of enormous snowflakes that plummeted like feathered bullets to the earth. A cold wind stirred up those bullets, driving them at a mean angle. In moments, Garnet was sheer ice from head to shoe. She had never felt so cold.

"This is mighty disagreeable country," she shouted over the gusty wind.

"You haven't seen nothing yet. Wait until you see a full-fledged Montana blizzard."

With any luck, she thought, secretly happy.

Now, when exactly did she start *hoping* she'd be stuck here all winter?

* * *

Gunslingers. Outlaws. Scar-faced men wearing guns. Virginia City's noisy, filthy, muddy main street wove like a snake through the hilly town. Despite the late hour, Garnet was not surprised to see the flock of men milling from one saloon to another.

The streets were jammed with life. Merchants on corners, men in the streets, soiled doves hanging out of second-story windows. And it was noisy. Men yelled above the clack and rattle of wagons, horses whinnied their opinion of the muddy streets, and the calls of the soiled doves rang like bells above the din.

Garnet felt out of place, a lone woman on the dangerous street of this frightening mining town. She might have been terrified, but walking beside Wyatt with his capable look, his steely strength, and his lethal black eyes scared off any trouble.

Shivering and miserable, Garnet never thought she would feel so relieved to touch the ground again. She dismounted in the livery, with Wyatt's hand on her elbow to steady her. She was exhausted from the long ride, and her legs ached. Her fanny hurt even worse! If only she could just lie down in one of the fresh clean stalls and close her eyes for a moment.

But she could not afford to rest. She had a sister to find, so she stood huddled, dripping wet, while Wyatt gave explicit and very long-winded instructions to the stable boy on how to care for his muddy, thoroughly soaked mare. Apparently the horse was expensive, and he seemed to be very attached to it.

After ascertaining that a young couple matching Lance and Golda's descriptions had stabled a donkey in that particular livery, Garnet led Wyatt back out into the night. The stable boy didn't know where the man and woman had headed, but they were talking of marriage. Small groups of men wandered by, looking for excitement. The snowfall had little effect on the town's nightlife.

Garnet couldn't stop shivering. Or panicking. She knew she should find clean clothes and dry off, maybe eat a warm meal. She knew this cold night could put a chill in one's lungs, but she had no time to spare. Golda was about to make the worst mistake of her life.

"Let's try Madame Dumont's," Wyatt spoke in her ear, his breath hot. "One of the ministers often hangs out there in the doorway, preaching against all the drinking and gambling. If he's there, we can ask him where to start. And if not, Madame Dumont will know."

"I'll not set foot inside a gaming house!" Garnet bristled, folding her arms and planting her feet. "Well, maybe to find Golda."

Wyatt laughed. He reached out his hand, big and gentle. She stared at it, considered all he was offering.

Help. Friendship. Support. Tentatively, she placed her hand in his. His skin felt cold from the temperature, but Wyatt's touch was enough to warm her. Light from two neighboring saloons spilled onto the street, catching the angle of his jaw and the line of his nose.

So handsome. Garnet couldn't stop admiring him.

"Don't worry." Wyatt tucked her hand against his side, drawing her closer. "If Eleanore Dumont doesn't know where the ministers are, no one does."

"You sure seem to know this town. Have you spent that much time prospecting in this country?"

"No. I was a deputy here."

"You?" Why, that couldn't have been long ago. Anyone could see the town had grown up out of the wilderness overnight. "Why did you leave a steady-paying job to hunt gold? It doesn't make any sense to me."

"Let's just say it was an opportunity I couldn't let pass me by." His mouth twisted into a frown, not a smile, and his eyes were troubled.

Had something happened? She wondered. Some event that had hurt him? Then she remembered his wife, the one who left him, no, divorced him. Why would anyone leave this fine man? Garnet could not stop the growing dislike for Wyatt's former wife. Why, she must have been an addlepated toad not to want him. Anyone could see how much he still hurt. And how good a man he was, deep down, beneath all his tough exterior.

He leaned close. "I've put half of the men on this street in jail for one reason or another. Drunkenness, brawling, that kind of thing."

"Looks like some of them are still at it." She watched a pair of men fall out of a saloon's open doors and tumble onto the boardwalk, fighting and cussing.

Wyatt laughed. "I guess I made little difference in the long run, no matter how hard I tried." The shadows in his eyes were gone, replaced by crackling humor. "See? My steady job turned out to be just as unproductive as hunting for gold. Maybe less."

"You're a good man either way," she declared without doubt, deep and true.

Wyatt Tanner was the best man she'd ever known. He walked with confidence, his shoulders wide, his chin set, and an easy command in his stride. Whether he wore his miner's Levi's and a simple cotton shirt or a deputy's badge on his chest, she was proud to be seen with him.

Wyatt led her through the storm and into the grandest establishment Garnet had ever seen. The heated air washed over her. Chandeliers winked overhead, catching and throwing light into the wall of mirrors that glittered behind the expansive bar. Decanters glistened from their places on the fancy shelves. Fine wood tables and chairs were occupied with neatly dressed men, who gambled in low, quiet voices.

An elegant woman in luxuriant silks stepped into the room. Wyatt leaned close to whisper in Garnet's ear. Agreeing to stay by the door and out of trouble, she watched him cut through the peaceable crowds to the fascinating Madame Dumont. Something stuck hard like a knife in her belly. She watched the sophisticated-looking woman, a woman of the world, cast a welcoming smile at

Wyatt. The two spoke warmly like old friends reunited.

Garnet looked away. She wasn't jealous. She wasn't! No, that stab in her chest had to be hunger. That's all. They had missed supper, deciding not to stop on the trail.

Wyatt wove back toward her, his eyes bright and his smile wider than before he had talked to the beautiful and sophisticated woman. Garnet felt plain in comparison.

"The only minister likely to be working this late is the one who lives on the north side of town." Wyatt reached out and covered her hand with his bigger one.

"Then let's hurry!" Desperation drove her. What if they were too late? Garnet pulled him out onto the crowded street. "Which way is north?"

His rich chuckle warmed her in the way nothing could. "Left."

The streets were crowded, and she felt like a trout charging a river in spring flood. Her hand stayed tightly on Wyatt's as she led the way through the masses of men and brightly clad working girls. Urgency enveloped her. They had to hurry. She could feel it deep in her heart. They were running out of time.

She blinked hard against the falling snow, and cold air burned in her lungs. She searched the streets as she ran, scanning any number of strange faces, desperately hoping she would spot Golda and Lance in the crush of people. Hoping they had not found a minister yet.

"Here!" Wyatt tugged her off the main street and down a dark alley. Deep ruts had filled with ice and water, and without light gleaming from the business windows, she couldn't see a thing. The earth gave out beneath her and she fell in a deep puddle, wetting her skirts and her foot all the way up to her knee.

He caught her elbow and gently helped her up. "Are you hurt?"

"I don't think so." Her chest twisted at the concern in his voice. She limped onto safer ground.

"It's the house on the left," he directed.

The little shanty, small and boxy, had one curtained window that shed a meager bit of light into the alley. She tugged Wyatt after her and bounded up the front steps. Fearing the worst, she knocked loudly on the door. *Please, don't let us be too late.*

Her heart pounded hard, once, twice as she waited for someone to answer the door. It gave her plenty of time to imagine the worst. Perhaps Golda and Lance had already been here to make arrangements for a wedding tomorrow. What if they were sharing a hotel room?

The door flung open. A plump woman stepped into the lamplight and peered out into the night. "Another couple in love wanting to get married. My, what a busy night. Otis will be with you right after he joins these nice young people in holy matrimony."

CHAPTER ELEVEN

Wyatt watched Golda whirl from her place before the minister. He wasn't surprised to see rebellious rage souring the girl's face. There was no doubt Garnet loved her sister, or she otherwise wouldn't have a single motive in trying to save the girl from a foolish fate.

Lance Lowell didn't have more than a few ounces of gold to his name, was too lazy to work his claim, and was in debt all around town.

The kindly minister took one look at Garnet pushing her way into his parlor and blanched. "Miss," he called nervously from his place before the mantel with the wooden cross on it, "you'll have to wait until I'm done."

"Garnet!" The plump girl puffed up like a rebellious chick. "I am a grown woman and you no longer have any say over me or my life."

"Why, I—"

"Look at you!" Golda gestured at Garnet's clothing. "You look about as attractive as a drowned cow in a flood. I've never seen you look so disheveled. You're just jealous, that's what this is about. You know you will never have a man fall in love with you the way Lance has fallen in love with me."

"Is this how Lance has influenced you? To turn against your own sister?" Garnet halted halfway across the room, obviously torn and confused.

Wyatt pushed at the door, ready to step in and stop the argument. But the kindly minister's wife called him a ruffian and tried to shut the door in his face.

He could only hear Garnet's voice as he wrestled to open the door and step inside to save her.

"Please, Golda. Listen to me. I just want you to stop and think about what you're doing."

"You just don't want anyone to be happy because you can't be." Golda's chin bobbed upward, hatred boiling in her eyes. "You want me to be as unhappy as you."

"That's enough!" He forced his way into the parlor and saw Garnet in the lamplight, looking a little worse for the wear.

The ride had been hard. Her cloak and the hem of her dress were stained with mud from the trail. Her bonnet now hung limp and lifeless by its strings from her neck, and her hair fell in a rumpled tangle down her back. Yet she looked sensual and passionate, a real beauty in comparison with her sister's superficial looks.

"It's too late anyway." Golda's face wrinkled into an unattractive grimace. "I'm already married and I don't need either one of you."

Need. As if people were only to be used and tossed away when someone better—or more gullible—came along. Wyatt's mouth soured. His mother had been that way and so had his former wife, who threw away his love as if it were of no great value.

Garnet's heart sank. "Is it true? Is the ceremony finished? Are we too late?"

The squinty-eyed minister nodded. "I just pronounced them man and wife. The groom was about to kiss the bride."

Golda's eyes flashed. "You can't do anything now, big sister. Lance and I are truly wed."

"Then I wish you well." Garnet's voice was quiet, but thick with unfallen tears. "I didn't mean to be unkind. I only wanted to protect you. That's all I've ever done. I hope you understand. I was trying to do my very best."

"I doubt that," Golda challenged.

But even now Garnet refused to lash out, refused to hurt the sister she loved. Garnet Jones was nothing like most women Wyatt knew, nothing like the one who had broken his heart. She was everything he could believe in, everything he could ever want. Somehow, Garnet had come to mean more to him than anyone or anything in his life.

He set his hand on her slim shoulder. She gazed up at him with hurt in her eyes. His chest ached for her, and he pressed a kiss to her forehead before leading her to the door. The minister's wife rushed to open it, and they stepped out into the night.

"She doesn't want me." Tears choked Garnet's words. She stepped out into the slick street, dusted with glistening snow, her chin up and her spine pole-straight.

"She'll come around. She's just trying to grow up." He drew Garnet against the nearest building. Just enough light fluttered down from an upper story window so that he could see the pain on her face.

"I wish . . ." Her face crumpled, and she said nothing more.

"You did what you could to care for someone you loved, Garnet. You are a good person."

"How would you know?"

"What does that mean? I used to be a deputy. I know what a bad person looks like."

"Like you?" A glimmer of humor in her watery eyes.

He laughed, so she would feel better. "Yes. Gruff. Alone. Has a dirty coffeepot."

"Not anymore."

"No. You changed that." He dared to reach out and draw her hard against his chest. Their sodden clothes squished as their bodies met. She felt so good there, against his chest, in his arms, tucked beneath his chin. "Besides, don't give up all hope. Golda's marriage might work out. Who knows? If it doesn't, then she can come home to you in Willow Hollow and try to apologize for what she said. Marriages start and end all the time around here and nobody pays them much mind."

"Oh, that makes me feel better." But she almost smiled. "You make me feel a whole lot better."

"Tell you what. It's snowing like the dickens out here, in case you haven't noticed. Why don't I go find us a hotel, dry clothes, and a hot meal? When was the last time someone took care of you?"

"Why, it was you. Right now. And earlier today, when you bought the horses and supplies and I came to town and everything was all ready for us. And before that, when you bought me coffee."

"Then I've started a tradition I don't want to break. Let me take care of you tonight, Garnet. Come with me."

As she gazed up into his eyes, all tears and open heart, he thought she was going to say no. Then she smiled in the most beautiful way and made all his senses spin.

* * *

Garnet tried to keep a hold of her emotions as Wyatt booked her a room and asked that both a fire be lit and a bath be filled for her. A hot bath, just as he had promised. Her entire heart lit with a brightness she'd never known.

He stayed behind in the lobby, his black gaze unreadable as he told her to follow the rail-thin youngster upstairs. His tender voice, low and promising, echoed in her mind. This was no cheap hotel, she discovered as she stepped into the room.

She'd never seen such comfort. The carpet was as soft as wool, clean and sedate and elegant. And the wallpaper, why, she'd give anything to have such a beautiful floral pattern in shades of forest-green and raspberry in her house. Two upholstered wing chairs were set a comfortable distance from a stone fireplace, and the rich curtains matched the quilt on the wide bed.

A steaming tub sat in the corner of the room, and white fluffy linens were stacked on a nearby bureau. Her valise was on the trunk beside the carved wardrobe, although it was wet through from the trip. She immediately unpacked, hanging her dress and nightgown and underthings in the wardrobe, hoping they would be dry by morning. Only then did she strip out of her wet clothes and slip into the deep steaming water.

Soothing heat lapped at her skin. The cold in her bones and the hurt in her heart melted as she sank down to her chin. The water was scented with lavender; it filled her head and eased away the last of her worries.

She'd done everything she could for her sister, her father, her family. It was time to take care of herself.

She leaned back and closed her eyes. Slowly the soreness eased from her muscles and her fanny from riding that saddle astride all evening. She felt like a new woman, free of old responsibilities and heartaches.

A light knock rapped on her door.

"It's me." Wyatt's familiar voice mumbled through the thick plane of wood. "I picked up some things for you."

"What things?"

"New clothes. Yours are wet. I had to guess at the size. Let me in."

"But I—" She couldn't very well hop out of the water and answer the door without a stitch of clothing on. She stretched for a towel and stood. "Just a moment."

"Sure, go ahead and tease me. I know you're naked."

"Wyatt! You think you're funny, but you aren't. Just a minute." She stepped out of the tub with a splash. Water sluiced down her legs and puddled on the floor. She dried herself as fast as she could. The soft towel felt good along her warm skin.

"Hey, let me in. I won't mind if you're naked."

"You're a man bound for disappointment." She wrapped the luxurious towel around her, careful to cover every bit of her breasts she could. Unfortunately, it wasn't enough. She looked like those women who danced on tabletops in saloons. Well, it couldn't be helped.

Holding the towel together, she padded to the door. "I'll just open up so you can slip the package through."

"Not a chance, lady." His voice was muffled by the wood door. "You'd better let me in if you want to wear dry drawers tonight"

"Now you're resorting to threats and bribery."

"Or force if I have to." Trouble rang in his voice, the sort of trouble she was starting to like. The hinges creaked. "Open the door."

She did. He towered above her in the hallway, all dark eyes and smile. Her heart missed a beat.

"This is for you." He handed her a wrapped bundle.

"You can come in if you promise to behave. Oh, you're still in your wet things."

"Don't worry, I'm tough." His gaze snared hers as he stepped through the open door. Just his magnetic presence made the cozy room shrink. "I think I wasted my gold dust buying you clothes. You look awfully good in that towel."

Garnet blushed, aware she was giving Wyatt a healthy view of her cleavage. And her legs. Goodness. Answering the door had been a very bad idea. Especially since the package was heavy, requiring both hands, and she could feel the towel beginning to slip. It was coming loose!

She dropped the bundle and caught the towel just as it slid open. Her new clothes hit the floor with a thud, and she looked up into Wyatt's laughing eyes.

"I saw something I shouldn't have," he confessed.

She felt her face flame. "Not another word. Forget whatever it was you saw."

"That is a mighty big request."

She never should have invited him in. It was plain as day. What was he thinking? Worse, what had he seen? No, she didn't want to know.

He swept off his battered hat and crossed the room. He knelt before the fire. She admired the strength in his iron-hard arms as he reached for a log and fit it into the snapping flames.

"Aren't you going to see what I bought you?" His dark gaze met hers, and a knowledge winked there. The memory of what he'd seen when her towel had slipped.

Oh, he was never going to forget that. Her face flaming hot, she ducked her chin and retrieved the fallen package. It was held together by white twine. She untied the string and the brown paper fell open.

"Wyatt. I—" Words failed her. She simply forgot to breathe at the sight of the soft flannel nightgown with fine lace trimming and pearl buttons. "I've never seen such fine things."

Her rough fingers traced the gleaming buttons. She couldn't be expected to sleep in such a garment. And the dress! A lake-blue calico with sprinkles of small, darker blue flowers. Satin ribbons and lace and buttons in the shapes of blueberries garnished the dress. She opened her mouth but no sounds came out. She could only stare at Wyatt's gift, at this expensive, ready-made dress of such a quality fabric.

She heard his footsteps on the floorboards, as he approached. Beneath the towel her body quivered. His hands cupped her shoulders and she melted at his touch.

"I want to see you in it." His voice caressed the back of her neck.

She forgot how to breathe. She could only nod and he stepped away, leaving her tingling body confused and aching for his heated touch.

"I'll turn my back. I won't peek, I promise."

"You could step out of the room," she said instead.

Amusement flashed in his dark eyes. "Yes, but I don't want to leave you."

For the life of her, she couldn't think of what to say in response. He simply turned around, leaving her stammering like a fool. She had no choice. The towel hit the floor and she pulled on the lace-edged drawers she found folded in the bottom of the package. Then the matching camisole. Her hands trembled as she unbuttoned the front placket of the beautiful dress.

What was she doing? Accepting a man's gifts, dressing with him in the same room. She felt giddy, light-hearted, strangely dizzy. She was having fun, that's what this feeling was. For the first time in more years than she could remember, since before Ma had fallen ill, she had no responsibilities, no obligations heavy on her shoulders.

Anticipating the night yet to come, she pulled the dress over her head and settled the skirt on her hips. It felt odd without petticoats, but free, too. She busied herself buttoning the bodice. This dress ought to make even someone as plain as her pretty. Excited for Wyatt to see her, she took a shaky breath. "You can turn around."

He did. His gaze slid from her face down the entire length of her dress. A broad grin played across his mouth and reached all the way up to his eyes. "Blue is becoming on you. You should wear it more often."

"I think I will." Garnet felt as if a fairy's spell had changed her from a toad into a princess. "Thank you, Wyatt. It's the dress."

"It's you." He stared at her and said nothing for a moment. "Are you feeling up to a meal? We can go back to Eleanore's place. Great food and the safest spot in town. No gun-fighting allowed."

Garnet smiled. He was going to buy her dinner. No man had ever offered to do that before. "I would be honored to be seen in your company."

"You just don't know my reputation around this town." He stepped closer. His eyes had changed. He no longer looked lost; there were no shadows. Only laughter and affection and a spark of something so honest she could not force her gaze away.

"I don't care about your reputation." She lifted her face in a challenge, or perhaps in invitation. "I only care about you."

Like the last of winter's snow at the sun's touch, Garnet's whole heart melted. Wyatt could see it in her eyes, like ice cracking on a pond. Some distant, protected part of her simply gave way, relaxed, and it occurred to him then he had never seen a more beautiful woman. Her lustrous black hair hung wet and seductive down her back, but small wisps had dried in airy curls about her face.

He closed the distance between them. It took so little to move his hands to her upper arms. When he found her mouth with his, she met his kiss willingly. All tender heat and velvet caresses. How he wanted her. He cupped her chin with one hand just to touch her, just to hold more of her while his lips tasted hers.

The night stood still. The bustling noise outside the window faded. Even the steady beat of his heart stopped as Garnet's mouth shifted beneath his, tentative, innocent. He tipped his head to take more of her, to run his tongue along the delicious seam of her lips, over the smooth surface of her teeth, testing the heady feel of her tongue twining with his. She lifted a small, warm hand to his jaw.

A groan of desire started down deep in his belly and worked its way up. He wanted all of her. Here. Now. For as long as he could have her. He didn't care when or how. He only knew that he had never wanted anything more than he wanted Garnet. And he knew she felt it, too. He knew by the rough way her breath fanned his cheek and how her body leaned into his invitingly.

Oh. The groan tore from his throat and he eased her back onto the large bed centering the room. She slipped back willingly, clinging to him, refusing to interrupt their kiss, all lips and teeth and tongue. Wyatt's whole world tilted from a rough, solitary existence to that of need. He needed her touch. He needed her body. Most of all, he needed her affection.

As if she sensed that, Garnet slipped her hands over his chest, skimming across his skin. Without thinking, he ran his right hand over the soft cotton of her bodice to cup her perfect breasts. Soft, warm, like nothing in his life, nothing in his world. She was this magic that changed his shack into a home, his loneliness into need.

He fumbled with tiny buttons and soon her bare breasts were filling his hands.

"Oh, Wyatt," she breathed in a sigh, lost, dazed, as spellbound as he. He lifted his mouth from hers and trailed wet, sensuous kisses down her throat. She groaned freely just as he knew she would when his mouth closed over her budded nipple.

"Oh, *Wyatt.*" Her voice changed.

She must feel it too, he thought. This tumbling rush of passion. The clench of hard need. He ran his tongue over her breast, teasing, tasting, caressing.

"*Wyatt.*" She planted both palms flat against his forehead and shoved hard. His head snapped away from her breast and he stared at her, panting.

"What?" He didn't mean to sound so irritable.

But looking into her frightened eyes, he knew what he had done. It had been too fast for her. He stood. He ran his hands through his tangled hair, and he could hardly turn to look at her for the way it made his heart hurt. Silence ticked by and she sat up on the bed, holding closed her new dress, a disheveled, attractive, amazing woman gazing up at him with tears in her eyes.

"I'm sorry," he choked out. How had he lost control? How had he been so misguided as to think a woman this fine would want a man like him?

"I'm not. I'm just not used to such feelings." Her chin was bowed and the little bit he could see of her face was bright red, flushing with embarrassment. No, desire.

He held out his hand. He didn't deserve her, could never deserve her, but how he wanted her. "Let's go hunt us down some supper."

"Even at this late hour?" Her chin trembled as she gazed up at him. Vulnerability and want shone in her eyes.

"Even at this hour," he confirmed, for the gold town of Virginia City never slept.

"Then I will allow you to buy me supper, Mr. Tanner." She held out her arm. "As long as you behave like a gentleman. In public."

In public. Why, she hadn't said one word about how he should behave in private.

* * *

What had she done? Garnet wondered over her steak supper. She'd become thoroughly infatuated with Wyatt.

"You haven't touched your glass of wine," he observed from across the intimate table in the corner of Madame Dumont's establishment.

"I've never sampled spirits before."

"A little wine never hurt anyone."

He was teasing her. No, he was tempting her. Garnet took a bite of her baked potato. She studied the wineglass, glittering in the candlelight. "I've been adventurous so far. Why should I stop now?"

"That's my philosophy."

She had already panned for gold, ridden astride, and nearly

stripped herself naked just for more of a man's touch. What was a little alcohol compared to that?

She sampled the wine. Liquid sweetness tumbled across her tongue. "This is delicious. I like it."

She was learning she liked a whole lot of things.

A man stepped up to the table. "Tanner. The boys and I have missed you at our regular games."

"Been busy up north." Wyatt's forehead crinkled and his jaw tensed, but he stood and shook the stranger's hand with great gusto. "It's good to see you, Reardon."

"Who's the beautiful lady?" Reardon studied her. "Are you getting soft in your old age? None of us can remember you keeping the company of a woman."

"There's a first time for everything."

Garnet liked knowing Wyatt hadn't taken many women out to dinner as a regular habit in his life as a deputy.

"Ma'am." Reardon tipped his hat. "We were hoping you would play a few hands with us. Perhaps your lady will be understanding."

"Understanding?" Wyatt's gaze met hers. "I'll let you know. Tell the boys hello for me."

"Will do." Reardon backed away. "Ma'am."

"You used to spend a lot of time gambling?" Garnet asked over the rim of her wineglass.

Wyatt curled his fingers around the knife's wooden handle. He concentrated far too hard on cutting his steak. "Saloons and gaming halls are always a good source of information for a lawman."

"Sure. I believe that."

"You wouldn't believe what men will let slip with enough whiskey under their belts. I've solved some of my most difficult cases that way—" He stopped. "Besides, it helps to have something to do with your nights when there's nobody at home to miss you."

"Were you going to play poker tonight?"

He set down his knife. "Not without you."

"What if I don't play poker?"

"You didn't drink alcohol until a few minutes ago." His thumb caressed the back of her hand, soft circular strokes that made the surface of her skin heat and thrum wherever he touched her.

"I didn't used to do a lot of things until I met you. You, Wyatt Tanner, have been a very bad influence on me."

"I'm trying." He leaned close. "I bet you couldn't outsmart all those men and win some of their money."

"Outsmart them?" Garnet turned to study the table. "What does that have to do with playing poker?"

"It's a game of strategy. Of thought." He knew darn well he was tempting her, teasing her with the one thing that would spark her interest. "You probably aren't smart enough to outthink those men. They are bankers and merchants. They're pretty clever."

She could see he was baiting her, but her intelligence was one thing she had to defend, at any cost. "Are we making a wager, Mr. Tanner?"

"We are. I bet you can't win a single hand."

"And I bet I can."

"Then we'll need something to wager with. Something of great value."

Her stomach fluttered. "What do you have in mind?"

"The hotel only had one room left when we arrived."

"Only one? But where—"

"I made arrangements at the stable. I've slept in worse places." He held out his hand in a challenge, a wager of honor between two intelligent people. "I bet the bed. Whoever wins gets to sleep in it tonight."

She knew perfectly well what was on his mind, but Garnet Jones was not a woman who backed down when she was sure to win.

"You're on, Mr. Tanner." And they shook on it.

CHAPTER TWELVE

"It's your turn," Wyatt mumbled in her ear.

She knew. She was just trying to decide what to do. Four well-dressed men watched her carefully over the table, amused that a woman of such little skill had joined them. Oh, she knew they had agreed to this only to have Wyatt at their table.

These men were far too confident, she decided. They did not think she could win. Garnet consulted the scrap of paper on which Wyatt had written the rudiments of the game. A flush. That's what she had. A consecutive hand of hearts from five to nine.

Bluffing, that's what Wyatt called it. She caught him now, his own cards hidden in his palm, watching her face. Why, he was trying to beat her, too!

"I'm not sure what to do," she lied. "I guess I might as well do what everyone else is doing."

"If you aren't sure, you may want to sit out the hand," Reardon said from across the table, speaking as if she were an eight-year-old.

She picked up three of the same color chips she'd seen Wyatt use and tossed them onto the growing pile in the center of the table. "I'll see you." And nervously bit her lip.

Now the betting had gone to the man at her other elbow, who raised the ante even higher.

Goodness. How much were those little chips worth? Wyatt hadn't said when he'd poured nearly a dozen into her hands.

"I'll call." Reardon puffed on his cigar, eyes ambiguous.

Wyatt laid down his cards. Pairs of tens. Reardon laid down his. A flush of clubs from four to eight.

"You're getting rusty, Tanner." Reardon laughed as he reached for the pot.

"You forgot about the lady." Wyatt's rum-smooth voice rumbled over her.

"What do you have, dear?" Reardon asked, speaking as if she were too simpleminded to understand.

But she smiled. "A good enough hand to beat you."

When she laid down her cards, the men—all but Reardon—burst into laughter. Winston at her left patted her on the back with bold congratulations. Beeks across the table lifted his shot glass in a merry toast. But Wyatt, he just looked at her with eyes so full of pride, it made her heart stop.

"Well done," he said, and those were the sweetest words she had ever heard. His praise, his regard meant the world. "Don't forget to take your winnings."

"All that?" She stared at the big pile of chips. Gosh, she'd never imagined she might win money. She'd only wanted to prove to those men she wasn't easy to out-smart.

It was Wyatt who leaned forward and scooped up the chips for her.

"It's my deal," Beeks announced as the room grew quiet. "Seems our little lady is gathering some attention."

It was true, Garnet realized when she looked up. Many bystanders had collected a small distance from the table to watch the game. Many of them were handsome young men. Some smiled at her. Goodness. Were they flirting with her?

"She's just suffering from beginner's luck." Reardon tapped the ashes from his cigar. "We'll win back our money and they'll lose interest."

Her pride prickled. When she looked at her cards, she was disappointed. It wasn't the hand she had hoped for.

"Three cards, please," she told Beeks, who dealt her three more. That was much better. But to fool her fellow players, she tried to look really disappointed.

"You can stop anytime you want," Wyatt whispered in her ear. "But of course everyone will think you won because you were lucky, not smart."

She laughed. "I know what you're doing, Wyatt." He had

figured out a way to be with her and play poker with his buddies. Well, she couldn't fault him for it. She was having fun.

When everyone laid down their cards, she surprised them all again. Her pair of queens had them all beat, even Wyatt with his pair of jacks. Again, that pride gleamed in his dark eyes, and she felt happy. Truly happy.

She sipped her sarsaparilla and knew she would do anything just to see that look in his eyes, so beautiful and true, and all for her.

* * *

"I can't believe I did so well," she breathed as they burst into the room. Those poker chips were heavy in her reticule, jangling and clanging as she walked.

"I'm not surprised." Wyatt's dimpled smile took her breath away.

"I never thought I would have so much fun!" She'd lost a few hands, but won even more, and the thrill of trying to make the best of whatever hand she'd been dealt had grown on her.

"Now do you see why men gamble?"

"Well, they oughtn't gamble the grocery money away if they have wives and children." She couldn't stop herself, then she laughed. "Fine. It's a fun game. Especially when you win."

She upended her reticule and dumped out her chips onto the bed. "Let's see. Here are your chips back. Four each of the red, blue, and white."

He tried to decline, but she wouldn't hear of it. Soon, she was looking at a small pile that represented her winnings, maybe twenty-five or so. She'd earned this by her wits and her intelligence, however little it was. "How much money did I win?"

"Let me count it." He thumbed through the pile. "Five thousand, two hundred dollars."

"*What?*" Her knees buckled. "Stop joking with me, Wyatt. That isn't funny."

"It's no joke. You were in a high-stakes poker game tonight. No penny-ante players."

"*Five thousand dollars.* I have five thousand dollars. I can't believe it."

"You've earned enough money to go home in style. And then some."

That wasn't what she was going to say. But she could not deny the truth in his words. The joy in her heart ebbed, like foam from a midnight shore. She ought to be happy about the money she'd won, and she was. She was just more sad at the prospect of leaving Wyatt.

Then came his deep voice, soft as a caress. "Now that you're fairly wealthy, I hope you will still speak to a lowly prospector like me."

She tucked her bottom lip between her teeth, refusing to speak her feelings, refusing to meet his eyes.

He touched her chin with his thumb. "Can it be? Have you been rendered speechless?"

She blushed. "No, I just ... I want . . . Ooh." She laughed, a wonderful breezy sound that chased away the last doubts in his heart. She turned to untie her bonnet, and lamplight shimmered in the cascade of her ebony hair. She had left it down tonight, curled loose around her face.

He ached to wind his fingers deep into those midnight curls. How could he not remember the sweet aching brush of her kiss? Or the enticing taste of her breasts? How could he not want more of her?

When he spoke, his voice came gruff and scratchy. "With this snowstorm, the stages will shut down. Travel across the mountains would be too risky."

A soft blush colored her cheeks. How beautiful she looked. "I suppose I can't make any decisions until the snow stops."

"Yes." They would have this night together. He fought the urge to draw her to his chest, tuck her against his heart, and never let her go. She wasn't his to hold onto.

She took a breath, held it as if ready to change her mind. Then, she spoke. "I suppose we might as well stay here for tonight. Together. Since it's so cold out in that stable. I would hate for you to catch a chill."

Somehow she was in his arms. She felt like forever. She felt like home.

"I was betting you would invite me to stay," he whispered now, because he could not find his voice.

She gazed up at him, her smile mysterious. "I was betting, too." Her mouth opened, but she said nothing more. She didn't have to. He could read it in her eyes. She wanted him. The same way he wanted her.

The knowledge made him bold. He brushed her sweet mouth

with his. She tipped her head back, parting her lips. Moist and open, her kisses . . . and passionate, how passionate. His body responded to her. Desire and affection mingled together in a sweet burn, hotter than whiskey, brighter than anything he had ever known before.

"Wyatt." Her warm breath fanned his neck just above his shirt collar. Just when he expected her to tighten her hold on him, she took a step away.

"You don't like my kisses?" he asked.

"Yes, I—" She blushed, then covered her face with both hands. "I shouldn't be doing this, you know, sharing the night with you."

"Then you need to be sure it's what you want. I don't want you to have any regrets, Garnet. If you would rather, we don't have to be intimate. We can just sleep." He took a breath, hoping that wasn't what she wanted.

"I don't want to sleep."

"Are you sure?"

"Absolutely." The slight nod of her head made her lustrous hair brush over her shoulders, over her breasts. "I feel as if I've been waiting for you all my life."

"So do I." All the years of emptiness, of simply existing faded. As if they were two lost halves found, he stepped toward her, reaching out his hand. "I've never wanted a woman the way I want you."

"Oh." Great tears filled her eyes, brimming over. She could hardly see him, but she didn't need to. He was part of her heart, her soul.

His mouth closed over hers again, hard and possessive. The world faded until there was only him, the iron wall of his chest, the whisper of his breath mingling with hers, and his kiss. Oh, his kiss. She loved how his tongue brushed the inside of her mouth with velvet strokes.

Desire twisted through her, a desire that made her feel light and airy, like morning sunshine, like fluffy white clouds in an afternoon sky. Wyatt nibbled her chin, and she laughed. His hands brushed down her arms and, taking her hands, he backed her toward the bed.

She sat down and gazed up at him, at this man she cared for so much. He wanted her. The realization brought tears to her eyes and an ache to her heart. Anyone could see his honest affection.

Anyone could see how his hands shook when he knelt down to unbutton her shoes.

If she wanted to stop this, now would be the time, but Garnet could only smile at the man pulling off her shoes, then her socks.

"You have nice toes," he said.

"You're bluffing."

"Never when it comes to you." A grin touched the corner of his mouth and she kissed it, tasting that lopsided smile she adored so much.

Her heart had never felt this light, this carefree. Her breath caught when he sat on the bed beside her, the feather mattress dipping at his greater weight, tilting her toward him.

He laid his hand against her jaw, a tender touch that made her heart flutter. She wanted his touch. She wanted so much. He loosened her buttons. Feeling the gaping fabric, she laid back on the bed. He slid the dress from her shoulders and the sleeves down her arms. The material puddled around her waist, leaving only the camisole. He leaned on one elbow, gazing down at her, not at the lacy undergarment but at her face, her eyes.

She reached up and unbuttoned his shirt. Maybe it was too bold, but she wanted to see him. She wanted to touch him. The fabric parted to reveal his textured chest. Muscles contoured the length of his torso, so different from hers. Where she was soft, he was hard and muscled. His skin was brushed with a scattering of dark hair. She curled her fingers through that black mat.

"You aren't wearing all those underthings women usually wear." His voice came husky and low.

"My corset was wet from our trail ride."

"Then I only need to remove this and you'll be mine?" He tugged at her camisole strap.

She could only nod. He slid the straps from her shoulders, and material slipped over her breasts and bunched at her waist. Her heart stopped beating as she lay half naked before him, exposed to his scrutiny. She knew she ought to be embarrassed, but how could she be? Not when he was gazing at her as if she were beautiful, truly beautiful. He made her feel that way.

His callused hands smoothed gently over her breasts. Garnet shivered. He touched her and made fire. He kissed her and sparks turned into flames. Burning now, Garnet shivered when he cupped her breasts with his big hands, shaping her, caressing her, covering one peaked nipple with his mouth.

She gasped. Sensation rocketed through her and coiled low in her abdomen. Wyatt nibbled one breast and then the other, tugging deliciously on the aroused peaks. She closed her eyes and basked in the pleasure. If only she could keep her hands still. They swept over the curves of his muscled shoulders, down the hardness of his back, across the span of his chest.

Affection overwhelmed her, and she felt restless. Unable to simply lay still, Garnet wrapped her arms around his neck and arched her breast into his mouth. Groaning, he suckled harder. Sharp shafts of pleasure speared through her. She throbbed down low, where a hot dampness was collecting between her thighs. She shifted her hips, but the tightness in her abdomen only increased. She rained kisses along his forehead, then licked the crest of his ear. When he groaned, she did it again.

He chuckled and reached up to catch her mouth with his. Passion ruled this kiss. His tongue drove over hers with a rhythmic fierceness that matched the growing wildness inside her. Garnet held on, delighting in the feel of his hands caressing her breasts, then her ribs, then beneath the puddle of clothes at her waist.

"Take this off." His lips brushed her with words and heated breath. "I want to see all of you. I've been wanting it for so long."

"How long?" she asked. Lifting a hand, she brushed a lock of his soft, wayward hair from his eyes.

He grinned like a demon-man, like the very devil himself. "Since I first looked at your thigh."

"I was an injured woman."

"I couldn't help myself." His strong fingers grasped at the clothes separating them. "You were wounded and couldn't run from me."

She laughed. He was teasing her. "I can run away now."

"Do you want to?"

"No."

His eyes darkened. He pulled away her skirt and chemise with one swift tug. Garnet felt giddy and free and strangely breathless. Wyatt's eager hands grabbed hold of her drawers. As soon as she had loosened the ties, he slipped the garment down over her thighs, then her knees, then off entirely.

She lay before him utterly naked. Her breath caught, and she felt a little shaky, but with excitement, not fear. At the sight of

Wyatt gazing down at her with wonder bright in his eyes, she knew she had nothing to fear, nothing to be anxious about. He would not hurt her.

Their gazes met and held. She saw only him, powerfully strong, endlessly tender. He reached out to touch her hip, and she closed her eyes.

His fingers grazed her like the wind, light, teasing. But unlike a wind, his touch lingered, grew bold, and skimmed down the length of her thigh. Every place his fingers went, she felt a burning sensation along her skin, a sensation that didn't fade but kept expanding. Soon, her entire body felt on fire.

This pleasure was overwhelming. She shifted on the bed, restless beneath his touch. But Wyatt didn't stop. His daring hands skidded down and then up her legs. He lingered to brush slow caresses along the soft inner flesh of her thighs. Her entire body began to quake. She wanted more of his touch. So much more. She dared to part her knees, and his fingers didn't hesitate. He caressed a tingling trail closer to a very private part of her. A moan escaped her throat. A brilliant pleasure sliced through her suddenly, the way lightning cuts across the sky.

Garnet snapped her eyes open and stared at the man who kept caressing her. His persistent fingers probed her apart, spreading the dampness collecting there like dew. Desire coiled tight in her belly. Heat simmered in her veins. Those slow strokes continued, and she could only welcome his touch. She could not, would not move away. A searing hot pleasure more intense than pain snapped through every nerve in her body.

Garnet came up off the bed, sitting up in her surprise.

Wyatt smiled, his eyes appreciative. "I take it you liked that."

"Yes." So bold, she blushed. "I don't want you to stop doing that. But . . ." She couldn't dare ask such a question.

"What? Tell me, Garnet."

She swallowed, trying to find the words. She had read of the physical act, had unavoidably witnessed it on the farm, had even seen pictures of Grecian statues in books. But she had never seen a fully aroused man, and she had always wondered . . .

"I want to see you," she confessed.

A strange grin skidded across his lips. "Sorry. That's forbidden."

"Stop teasing me." Blood thundered through her aroused body. She was hot and quivering. How she wanted him. Just him.

"Then help me," Wyatt invited.

Her hands visibly trembled as she reached out. She unbuckled his belt with slow, uncertain fingers. He kept still, kneeling on the bed beside her. He didn't dare breathe when Garnet pressed her hand there, where that part of him ached to be touched. She met his gaze and he saw wonder shining in her eyes, half-hidden, mysterious, intangible.

In all the years since he'd been divorced, he had never taken such a risk as this. If he made love to her, then she had the power to hurt him. A wise man would stop, but he was not wise. Nor could he halt the feelings in his heart. He didn't want to. He wanted to love her, to make love with her.

He snapped open his trousers and pulled down his drawers too quickly, he feared, betraying too much emotion, too much need. But Garnet didn't notice. Her gaze was fastened on him, staring at his jutting hardness.

Her hand reached out. "Can I?"

Oh, he understood her question. His voice came out rough and raw. "Yes."

Her hand closed over him. He trembled, afraid to breathe, afraid to speak. He didn't want her to move away, to stop touching him. But his fears were unfounded. She knelt down for a closer look.

Garnet, the scholar, appeared to be taking careful notes.

"You're like velvet," she commented, brushing the tip of his arousal with a light finger. It might as well have been a hard, long squeeze for the jolt of sensation she caused. "And much larger than I would have guessed."

Wyatt smiled. He could have made a joke about that, but he didn't. He was afraid to ruin the moment. He didn't know how to say the words, how to tell her what was in his heart. Hell, he couldn't even tell her how she was everything to him.

Her hand enclosed over the length of his shaft. "Can we—"

"Yes," he interrupted.

She bit her lower lip to keep it from trembling, and he could see her need as great as his own. He caught her mouth with his, kissing her hard, daring to take her in his arms and press her down onto the bed.

"Do you want me inside you?" He had to ask, because if she was uncertain, if she wanted to stop, this would be the best time to do it. "I don't want you to ever look back on this with regret."

"How could I?" She brushed one hand against his cheek. It was the softest, most loving gesture he had ever known. "I could never regret knowing you." She gazed up at him hopefully, as if she were unsure he felt the same way.

How could he not? Wyatt felt a great tearing in his chest, a great wash of emotions he kept so carefully buried away. He kissed her with the strength of those feelings, determined to make her know just how much he cared for her.

He touched her, and she moaned. He laid his knee against her thighs and she parted for him. Her kisses were as frantic as his. Her arms wrapped around his back and she pulled him to her. Desire warred in his blood. His shaft nudged her swollen softness, and she smiled. She kissed him with that smile and squirmed beneath him. He wasn't alone in his needs, in his wants.

He reached down to trail kisses along her mouth. Her tongue lashed up to catch his, and she arched her hips. Her message was clear. So, he did what she wanted and pressed into the resisting heat of her body.

As he entered her, her eyes widened. She gazed up at him, her mouth parting, her breath held. He waited for her to adjust to the feel of him.

"Are you all right?" he asked.

"Never better." They were nearly nose to nose. She could see so much of his eyes, not just the chocolate flecks buried amid the black of his irises, but the emotion. This meant something to him, too. She could feel his hot hardness nudging her apart. She felt as if there were too much of him, so very much of him. It didn't exactly hurt, but it wasn't comfortable, either.

"We'll go slow. There's no hurry." He kissed her again, deeply, passionately.

Her body adjusted to his thickness. He pressed deeper and she felt a quick pain. Before she could cry out, it was gone. He pressed kisses to her forehead, as if to comfort her. But she needed no comfort. She arched her hips to take more of him inside, and he filled her completely. She clasped her knees to his hips and held on. He moved, setting a rhythm of pulling away and thrusting deep that left her breathless and weak. She could only hold onto him, her arms tight around his back. Heaven could break apart and the world end, but still it couldn't stop this spiral of pleasure that tore through her, like something breaking loose. It tumbled away and rolled back again, higher, harder, hotter. Garnet took one tiny gasp and her body simply exploded.

Hard, searing spasms uncoiled in her tight muscles. The pleasure was like beauty, like the sharp edge of pain. It rolled over her with a force she couldn't stop, not even when he stiffened above her. He groaned and thrust heavy and fast. Still, her climax continued. She felt the warm throb as he spilled his seed, and still that rippling pleasure did not stop. Even when he relaxed over her, she kept moving against his thickness. Goodness, it felt so good she just couldn't stop.

Wyatt started to laugh. She saw only affection and acceptance and a whole lot of humor.

"Don't wear yourself out," he teased. "We can do this again."

"We have all night," she agreed, leaning back in his arms.

* * *

Garnet awoke tucked against the heat of his body. In a blink she knew they were both naked and that last night, before they fell asleep, they'd made love several more times. Contentment felt like sugar in her veins. Her body felt so relaxed and light. She stirred, and Wyatt mumbled in his sleep, reached out, and drew her back against him.

Goodness, the things she'd done with him ought to embarrass her in the light of day, but they didn't. She crept from his hold and out from beneath the covers, and met the new day shivering.

The air was cold. Was it still snowing? Part of her hoped so, the part that was sad at the thought of leaving. She hurried into her clothes, but not the dress she'd worn last night. She hung it up in the wardrobe, touching the beautiful fabric one last time. Wyatt had given her this dress. How she cherished it.

But today, in case she had to ride, she would wear something more practical. She chose the calico dress she'd packed. It was one of her prettiest dresses. She spent extra time with her hair, and in the end left it down and tied it with a length of lace.

"You decided to get dressed. I'm disappointed." He sat up in bed, the covers at his waist, showing off his bare chest. The memories of kissing that skin and other parts of him made her blush.

"I'm hungry," she explained.

"So am I. You didn't have to leave the bed to appease your

appetite."

"There are other hungers, Wyatt." Trouble was, she just couldn't think of any. Only the pleasures of last night, of the intimacies they'd shared, came to mind. Her blood heated just remembering.

"Then let me get dressed and join you. You shouldn't satisfy hungers all by yourself."

"Only certain hungers can be satisfied in public," she pointed out, earning his laughter.

She would love nothing more than to climb back into bed with him, but it was time to face the new morning and the coming day ahead. It took all her willpower to draw back an edge of the curtain and look out the window.

Silence beat in her heart, filled her from head to toe. Snow covered the silent town like a wool blanket, fuzzy and uneven and rippled from the night's wind. More snow fell in heavy flakes, descending from sky to earth.

She had another day of grace, another day of loving Wyatt. His hand fell on her shoulder, ever tender. He pressed a kiss to the back of her neck, and she knew he was thankful, too.

CHAPTER THIRTEEN

"**W**here are you going?" Garnet reached for the sheet and covered herself.

"To put more wood on the fire." Wyatt shot her a happy grin as he strode away. "I don't want you catching a chill."

"There isn't much chance of that. You've been doing a fine job of keeping me warm."

"A man has to do his best." He knelt down at the hearth. He began stacking split wood in the grate.

"So, that's the best you could do?" She settled the sheet over her breasts.

"What? You weren't satisfied?"

"Oh, I was satisfied." She laughed. "But we have yet to achieve perfection."

He stood, all male perfection as he strode toward the bed. "Are you suggesting we need to practice more?"

"Yes. I believe with a lot of practice and hard work you can improve your lovemaking skills."

He sat down beside her, the quirk of his brow hinting that he liked her suggestion. "Then I guess we had better get to work."

He swept her up into his arms and she laughed, leaning back, adoring the feeling of being held by him, loved by him. His mouth clasped over her breast and she held him there, kissing the crown of his forehead, pushing the sheets out of the way so they were flesh to flesh.

* * *

Wyatt watched Garnet sleep. It was afternoon, but they'd hardly slept last night and with all the lovemaking, they were both tired. Except she had a clear conscience, so she could sleep. He did not.

He brushed a finger along the edge of her heart-shaped face. She hadn't combed her hair in a while, and it fanned in unruly curls against the white of the pillow slip. She felt warm, soft as heaven, like everything good and gentle he didn't deserve and knew nothing about.

What did he know about love? About families? About caring for a woman? His only wife had found him in-adequate, confessing she'd never loved him. There was nothing to love. And in that he was like his father. He thought of his old man, violent when he drank, mean-spirited when sober. There had been nothing to love, nothing redeeming. Wyatt feared he was no different. He had spent his entire adult life using a gun to earn a living. He was little more than a paid killer, first when he'd served in the cavalry, then as a lawman, and now as a deputy marshal.

He pulled on his trousers and a clean shirt. The snow was letting up, falling straight from sky to the earth instead of sideways, driven by the wind. This was only the first cold weather of the season. The coldest weather was yet to come.

A knock on the door startled him. Garnet didn't stir and he hurried across the room to open it.

"Wyatt?" Beneath that black hat was a familiar face.

"Good to see you, Murphy."

"I heard from Reardon you were back in town. Did you find your brother's killer?"

Wyatt looked over his shoulder. Garnet was still fast asleep. He stepped out into the hall and closed the door. "Not yet. I've been making good progress in the case. Is the judge keeping you busy?"

"Too busy. We miss you at work."

"I don't know how much longer it will take." Wyatt thought of the woman on the other side of that door. Of the cabin they'd shared in Stinking Creek. Of the future they couldn't have. "Maybe another month or more. You can tell the judge I'm easy to find, if he needs me."

"Sure. I'll tell him." Murphy couldn't hide the teasing laugh. "You, a prospector. There's a stretch. You can't tell me everyone is believing it."

"Believe it." Wyatt again thought of Garnet. How would she feel if she ever learned he had been lying to her? She would understand, a part of him said. But another part knew better. Garnet's father lied to her all her life. She would not accept lies from any man. "I'm doing pretty well on my claim."

"Well enough to give up your job?" Murphy rubbed his chin.

"Maybe." Wyatt thought of the gold he'd carefully hid on the land that had been Ben's before he was killed.

"No one has tied you together with your brother?"

"No. I won his claim in a poker game. The next morning, when I went to interrogate the man, I found him dead in his tent."

"Someone from town wanted to keep him quiet."

"Exactly. I've been watching my back, but I haven't had the same trouble. And I won't as long as everyone believes my claim has played out."

Wyatt left a note for Garnet and went down to the dining room with Murphy. They talked more about the office in Bannack where they worked together, and Wyatt told Murphy, a good friend, more about his suspects and his leads. It was down to a few men. With patience, he would learn which was the one who had taken Ben's life for a sack of fifty-dollar gold nuggets.

When Murphy left, Wyatt felt troubled. He trusted his friend, he knew no one in the dining room had overheard what they'd been saying. His investigation was not compromised. But his conscience smarted. He had a job to do and had asked to do it because it mattered more than anything to him, but he was not the man Garnet thought. And he wasn't the man she needed him to be. Not only had he lied to her, he'd taken her virginity. She gave it willingly, but she didn't know the kind of man he truly was.

One thing was certain. Garnet must never know what he'd done to her, the lies he told, the man he was. She had to leave on the next stage out of town.

Garnet woke to a lonely room. Wyatt was nowhere in sight, but a merry fire crackled in the hearth and a note crinkled on the pillow beside her. She sat up to read it.

"Had to run some errands. Be back soon." She ran her fingers over the bold scrawl of his writing. Powerful, just like he was.

Well, she couldn't just lie about in bed all day. Not by herself, anyway. She pulled on her clothes, remembering Wyatt had been the one to undress her. Smiling, warm and content from their midday lovemaking, she ran a comb through her hair and tied it back with lace. All ready for a bit of errand-running. She really ought to get Golda a wedding gift, if she wanted to make peace. And she'd promised her sisters back home special gifts from Montana Territory.

But thinking of the gifts to be bought reminded her of leaving. Sadness crept into her heart at the thought of leaving Wyatt. After what they'd shared, it felt like she would be leaving a part of herself behind, the most important part. Did he feel the same way? He hadn't asked her to stay.

Her sadness grew with the knowledge. She walked to the window and pulled back the drapes. The snowy town was alive two stories below, the streets teeming with horse-drawn wagons and riders and merchants selling their wares. The snow had stopped.

It was time to make a decision. Time to make the biggest choice of her life. To walk away from this once-in-a-lifetime love, or to stay with Wyatt.

She glanced at the bed, sheets rumpled from their lovemaking. She remembered how he'd treated her in that bed, the tender touches, the gentle kisses, the way he clung to her so tight when he came. The affection had been honest in his eyes, and it hurt to look at it. Surely he loved her. Surely, staying would be the right choice.

It hit her in a flash, a sudden brightness of awareness that stole the beat from her heart. She loved Wyatt. Truly loved him. Would lay down her life and endure anything just to be with him.

The door flung open and there he was, striding through the doorway, all cocky confidence and strength. He tossed his hat on the bureau and slipped out of his coat. "You look beautiful."

Her heart twisted, glad he thought so. No other man had ever said those words to her. No other man made her feel beautiful.

"I brought you something."

"You did?" A gift. She saw the wrapped box in his hand, tied with a delicate blue ribbon. The same shade of blue as the dress he'd bought her.

"Go ahead. Open it," he urged.

Garnet lifted the present from his palm. It was small, like a jewelry box. Her heart skipped a beat as she untied the ribbon, then again when she unfolded the paper. She lifted off the box lid and could only stare. Inside lay a necklace glittering against a bed of dark blue felt, a gold locket in the shape of a heart.

"So you will always remember our stay in Virginia City." He brushed a hand along the side of her face, so tender she could not doubt his regard.

"I will never forget." How could she? How could she forget this man who had her heart? She took the necklace from the box and unclasped the beautiful linked chain. Wyatt moved behind her to secure it, and she admired the locket in the bureau mirror.

Then she caught his reflection in the glass and saw the shadows around his eyes and the tension in his jaw.

He had to tell her. Wyatt watched Garnet brush errant curls back from her eyes as she looked at a selection of women's scarves. Gifts for her sisters, she'd said. Did she intend to mail them home? Or take them back with her? How could he ask which? How could he tell her she would be better off going back to New York?

Her locket sparkled when the light caught it, a glimmering that could not rival her beauty. Her hair fell in soft curls down her back. She was all slender grace and laughing intelligence. When her gaze caught his across the shop, her smile made him miss his step.

He had to tell her. Yet he didn't know how.

"This is the first time I've been able to shop and not worry about sticking with my budget." Garnet bustled down the aisle toward him.

That five thousand dollars she'd earned playing poker had given her freedom. He understood that. He liked how this newfound independence erased the worry lines around her eyes and mouth. She looked like the young, vibrant woman she was, as fresh as morning.

"I think my sisters are going to love the scarves I got them. I would like to do a little more shopping. Do you mind?"

He read the deeper question in her eyes. The ticket office closed in ten minutes. Although tickets for the stage would be available tomorrow morning before departure time, he knew the significance of her avoidance. She didn't want to go home.

Tell her, just tell her.

"I need to pick up a few supplies to take back to town with me." His shanty at Stinking Creek and his ongoing investigation were waiting for him. Neither could break his heart, not the way Garnet could.

"Then shall we meet for supper?" Her voice almost trembled.

He could read her fears plain as day. He had the same worries, too, the same insecurities of being rejected, of not being lovable.

They had gone too far for him to pretend he didn't love her. Just the thought of her riding off on tomorrow's stage tore at his heart and left a wide-open emptiness. She could never love a man like him, he knew. And he didn't want to destroy that affection gleaming in her eyes, more precious than the rarest of diamonds. If she stayed with him, she would learn of his lies and his flaws.

"Supper sounds fine to me." *Tell her*, he told himself. *Better to lose her now before she has all of my heart.*

But it was too late, he knew. He loved her—completely, without a doubt, without reservation.

"I suppose you'll want to drink and gamble the night away," he teased her, just to see her smile.

He wasn't disappointed. "There is no way I am jeopardizing my winnings, even if I am pretty good at poker. Besides, I thought there was another game you liked playing with me."

"Believe me, loving you is no game." Not to him. Not that he should have told her that either. She already had too big a piece of his heart, held too much power to hurt him.

She smiled. Because of him? Or because she was simply happy with her new independence? He could not deny she was experiencing the world for the first time, tasting it like a hungry child in a candy store. He knew this time between them couldn't last. But he would savor every moment while he could. So when the nights were long and lonely and not even whiskey was a good companion, he would have her to remember. The blue of her eyes, the charm of her smile, the way she made him feel worthy and whole and loved. Especially loved.

* * *

It was a long, uncomfortable ride home. Snow fell in tiny little crystals and then turned to freezing rain as the morning progressed. The horses slid on the trail. Her slicker froze solid as a board. The reins froze to her gloves. But not even such miserable conditions could dampen Garnet's spirits.

Since that moment in the Virginia City millinery shop, Wyatt hadn't said another word about her leaving. On the contrary, he'd held her closer, loved her more openly, spoken to her more tenderly. He even had the hotel wrap and ship her gifts back home.

Since she would not be delivering them herself, she meant them to be Christmas gifts. She spent extra time buying silk scarves and silver bracelets, fabrics and lace goods. Even a belt and buckle for Ruby's husband. She took the time to send a letter, too, letting everyone back home know she was fine, but both she and Golda had fallen in love and would not be returning to Willow Hollow anytime soon.

Wyatt rode ahead of her, shoulders set against the weather, trailed by two packhorses, the second newly acquired, piled high with her purchases. She had taken the liberty of a few indulgences, since it wasn't every day she came across such a financial boon. Besides, she hadn't spent too much of her winnings, which were now earning interest in a savings account in a reputable Virginia City bank. Wyatt didn't seem to mind, even now when he had to slow down on the trail for the packhorses.

Excitement beat through her veins. It was really true. She was going to stay here for the duration of the winter. Oh, she had such plans. She would continue her cleaning business, of course. She would keep her tiny fortune tucked away in the bank. And think of what she could do with their cabin. Why, it would take only a bit of elbow grease and lumber to turn that shanty into a cozy home.

Cozy. She blushed remembering how cozy she had been with Wyatt last night, and again this morning before breakfast and while they were packing their bags. No, the ice didn't seem cold at all when she remembered how hot Wyatt could make her.

* * *

Wyatt sat in his saddle, but his oilcloth coat only protected him from the ice, not the cold. It drove into his bones as he rode straight into the north wind. With every step of his mare forward up the trail, his thoughts were on Garnet. Was he a fool for wanting her to stay?

His heart weighed heavily. All he knew is that he wanted her. A woman who didn't know the kind of man he was beneath the easygoing prospector's garb.

Snow began to sputter from the sky as twilight descended. By the time he could see the town's lights, dingy yellow spots in the thickening dark, the snow began in earnest. Only a few of the hardy miners were out on the street. He glanced over at Tent Row and saw the tent flaps tied down tight against the wind.

The shack was a lonesome sight sitting in a mire of snow-dappled mud. The mare nickered, knowing she was home and that oats awaited her in the clean dry stable. He patted her neck. She was a proud animal, purebred Arabian, and a good mount. He dropped to the ground and led her out of the bitter wind. Then he stepped back into the snow to help Garnet dismount.

"I'm frozen stiff." Her teeth chattered when she spoke and her breath rose in great clouds.

He lifted her down when she had trouble swinging her leg over the saddle. How wonderful it felt to have her in his arms, if only for a moment, as he set her gently on the slick ground.

"I'll get a fire lit. Let's just hope the canvas roof held." It had a small tear in it, which wouldn't support the additional weight of snow. He had the lumber for a new roof, which he would start building as soon as this weather broke. "First I have to care for the horses."

"Let me help. We had workhorses on the farm, great big Clydesdales." She took her gelding and the second packhorse by the reins and led them to the stable.

He laughed. Was there anything Garnet wasn't capable of? They made small talk while they rubbed the animals down. He liked how she worked right alongside him, and in no time the horses were snug and fed.

"I think we need a big pot of coffee," she said, as her hand sneaked around his.

He held her tight. "I get to make it."

"I am so cold I'm not even going to argue." Even in this miserable weather she could laugh, and he liked that. She was just the kind of woman a man wanted by his side. The kind he wanted day and night for the rest of his life.

"I'll kindle the fire if you grind the beans. We'll both be steaming hot in no time." She flung open the cabin door and froze. "Heavens. What—"

He stepped past her into the cabin. He saw it all in a glimpse— the table on its side, bedding and the straw from the tick tossed on the floor, the food thrown from the shelves, the flour and cornmeal sacks ripped open, the ashes dumped from the stove, and all of Garnet's personal effects strewn on the muddy earthen floor.

She reached for the chair, righted it, and sank into its solid seat. Someone had angrily trashed the cabin. No, searched it. But why? "Were they looking for gold?"

"Count on it." He marched straight to the stove and kicked it, furious at the mess. "Some people will kill unarmed men just to get their hands on it."

"Is it safe here?" She had never considered bandits might loot a person's home. Or perhaps take more than their gold. How terrifying.

"Safe enough." A muscle jumped in his tensed jaw, but the steady confidence in his gaze told her he would always be there to protect her.

"Is there a lot of murder around here?"

"Enough to make a man cautious, but no more. The town is very peaceable. Probably because the claims just aren't panning out."

"You mean there isn't enough gold to steal? But I found that nugget when we were at the creek. Aren't all the claims like that?"

"Staking out a claim is a gamble." He set the table back on its legs. "Not many claims pay out, or some men simply don't have the patience to work the land."

She bent to salvage enough clean bedding for the night, although some of it had lain directly on the muddy floor and would need to be washed. Some of the clothes were salvageable as well. She joined Wyatt in the silent task of righting the foodstuffs.

"What the hell is this?" His angry curse boomed through the silence. "That no good thief took all my whiskey bottles."

The destruction of their home left her feeling vulnerable. Garnet knelt before the stove and stacked the kindling. What truly mattered was that they were safe, that they hadn't been harmed in a robbery. And Wyatt's stolen gold, which was obviously what the trespasser had been looking for, could be replaced.

"The fire will soon be hot enough to boil coffee," she promised. "Looks like the thief left Mr. Carson's chocolates alone."

Wyatt set the grinder on the table, his eyes troubled, his powerful muscles tensed.

"We'll make it right, don't worry." She laid her hand on his and wished she could fix everything that had ever hurt him. Or ever would.

"I'm not worried, Garnet. I just want to know who did this." A deep worry furrowed his brow.

"It doesn't matter. Let them have all your gold. We have everything we need."

And it was true, she realized. All she would ever need to be happy was this one magnificent man.

* * *

There was so much sympathy in her jeweled blue eyes that Wyatt simply couldn't tell her the truth. Not when they shared a cup of coffee, not later when they finished straightening up the cabin, and not at supper when they enjoyed Garnet's delicious pancakes.

All he had to say was that he'd lied to her. That he wasn't a miner. That the thief was a murderer and was still looking for all of Ben's gold . . . and hadn't found it. He was more concerned the killer had discovered his true profession.

Yes, that was a real worry. He'd been able to conduct his investigation leisurely, watching those who never suspected he wasn't what he claimed to be. Maybe it had been a bad call that he'd left his marshal's badge in the far corner of the straw tick because he didn't want to take it with him. He didn't want to risk Garnet finding it.

And while he'd found his badge safe and sound in the tick where he'd left it, he couldn't be certain his identity was still a secret. Had the killer discovered it? Probably not, but the possibility troubled him.

They ate together as the night deepened and the snow on the canvas roof overhead stopped dripping and began to freeze. Then they did the dishes together. He dried while she washed. They talked over their home improvement plans. Garnet spoke knowledgeably of carpentry and wanted to help him with the roof. She would like a wood floor, she added. Dirt was cool in summer, but she wasn't overly fond of mud.

"Wait until it freezes," he teased.

She swatted him with soap bubbles and they laughed. She wanted a few windows, too. She'd noticed glass panes in Carson's general store. They weren't too expensive and would let in warmth from the winter sun. It would save on firewood, wood he would have to chop.

Wyatt emptied the wash basins for her. She liked a man who didn't mind domestic tasks. A warm feeling glowed in her chest from their closeness. It was nice sharing worries and work and plans. Very nice.

"It's getting late and we should get a good night's sleep." She dried her hands on a towel and granted him a shy smile.

"Do you think we can both fit in that small bed?" His wicked grin didn't fool her.

"Maybe if we cuddle really close."

"Let's find out." The air was so cold even in the cabin, his breath came out in great clouds. But his kiss was hot against her mouth and soon she was warm everywhere.

He turned down the lantern's wick so only a faint light brushed across the bed. He scooped her up in his arms and laid her across the mattress. He took off her shoes and tickled her toes. Laughing, he fell across her.

When his mouth found hers, Garnet's giggling was replaced by a throaty moan. She surrendered to him completely, closing her eyes and wrapping her arms around his neck. Sweet minutes passed while he kissed her. Already she was breathing fast and hard, knowing what was to come. His hand explored the sensitive skin of her neck, tracing a line from chin to collar. Then his lips followed, trailing delightful kisses down her throat.

"How do I get inside this dress?" he whispered.

"The buttons." She twisted away from him to reveal the small gray pearls marching up her back.

"I'm in the shadows. I can't see them."

"Then you'll have to go by feel," she teased.

The small bed was cramped. He jabbed her in the ribs accidentally with his elbow, then kissed the spot to make it better. She felt butterfly tugs at her buttons and desire curling around her spine. Cool air breezed across her back as the dress fell loose about her shoulders.

She rolled over and watched his gaze fall to her chemise-covered breasts.

"There's more clothing," he observed.

All she wanted was his hands and his mouth on her breasts. "Help me out of my chemise."

His hands fumbled with the wide muslin straps at her shoulders. The garment came away, exposing her red winter underwear. He groaned, then helped her remove that article of clothing, only to discover more.

"How many layers are you wearing?" he demanded, staring at her muslin-covered corset.

"You look completely shocked. Surely you've seen a simple corset before."

"Not in all my memory," he admitted, staring at the stiff, awkward garment that more closely resembled armor than underclothes. He didn't see the need to explain he'd never undressed Amelia, who was not happy to perform her wifely duties and, well, he just lacked experience with such mechanical-looking clothing. "How do I get it off? Do I need a wrench or a saw blade?"

She leaned on her side. "Try untying the laces."

"I think we ought to start a new rule." He pressed a moist kiss between her shoulder blades.

"What rule?"

"You are not allowed to wear these unbreachable undergarments." He tugged on the laces and they gave. "I need easier access."

Laughing, she threw her arms around his neck and buried her face in the clean scent of his half-unbuttoned shirt. He smelled deliciously male, like freshly sawed wood, winter air and horses. She breathed in, memorizing his scent. She couldn't get enough, touch enough, remember enough. Winter would end, like her stay here, and she wanted to tuck each precious moment into her heart to warm the cold, lonely evenings in Willow Hollow.

Her bared breasts, freed from the unending layers of clothing, firmed in the cool brush of the night air. Wind rustled overhead, and Wyatt ran his fingers along the outside curve of one breast.

Everywhere he touched her, she burned. The more he touched her, the more she wanted him. She ran her hands across his chest, down his abdomen and lower. Desire coiled tight in her belly. How she wanted him, how she craved the feel of him pumping and pulsing inside her.

Finally he moved between her thighs and sheathed his hot length inside her. She wrapped her body around his and gave herself up to the heat and the passion. It was more than physical joining, more than two individual people, greater than anything she had ever known. Her release crashed over her, rippling in great breathless waves.

When they were spent, Wyatt spooned his body around hers and tucked the muslin sheets and heavy wool blankets around them. Her head fit beneath his chin and his hand lay between her breasts, right over her heart.

Sleep came slowly, but it was the sweetest slumber she had ever known.

CHAPTER FOURTEEN

Garnet had never felt so invigorated. Perhaps it was the frosted morning air that greeted her, rousing her blood. Or perhaps it was this land itself, rugged and vital. But as she heated her wash water on the stove, she knew there was another reason.

The passionate night spent in Wyatt's arms.

She heard his hammer outside, ringing with each precise stroke. After her morning's work, she had agreed to join him up on the roof. He would need help laying the boards and sealing them with pitch. Tomorrow they could nail on the shingles. Already she could see how pleasant this cabin would be, just the two of them cuddling close through the long winter.

Contented with those romantic daydreams, Garnet gathered up the lye, her brush, her towels, and her bucket and headed outside. She had been up early cleaning what she could of the cabin. Now, all she had to do was her weekly outhouse cleaning, and then she could start on the laundry. Sweet Katy would soon be arriving to help out.

Snow had just started to fall in crisp, delicate flakes that stuck to her eyelashes and clung faithfully to the frozen ground. Wyatt was high up on the ladder, replacing a cracked board. He waved down to her, a smile bright on his cold-reddened face. "More cleaning?"

"Just getting the chores done. When you see Katy coming from town, let me know. I'll put on some water to boil. She's going to be helping me with the business."

"Where are you headed with that bucket of lye water? You'd better leave my stable alone."

"Really, clean a stable? Who ever heard of such a thing?" She tightened her hold on her scrub brush. "I am going to clean the privy."

"The outhouse?" He tipped his head back and laughed. "Really, Garnet, you've gone too far."

"I'm sure you've never cleaned one," she retorted, not at all surprised. "If you scrub it clean and add lye weekly, then it stays fresh-smelling and pleasant."

"Think of you to find a way to make the outhouse smell good." Wyatt laughed harder.

Well, who wouldn't clean a privy? Garnet flung open the outhouse door and lowered the bucket to the floor. She dunked her brush into the steaming lye water, knelt before the board seat and scrubbed with all her strength. The wooden bench wobbled, loosening more with each brush stroke.

How handy. She could slip the entire flat board off its wooden supports and take it outside. Then she could really get down on her knees and get the thing clean. There would be no awkward bending and no twisting to get into those dark corners.

Garnet set down her brush and began to tug. Finally it came loose, and she tipped the seat sideways to slip it out through the door.

But a shape in the shadows drew her back. Vermin? Stifling a scream, she picked up her brush. Then she realized the shadows between the boards didn't move.

What on earth? She leaned closer. Why, those lumps were little bags. She brushed one with her finger. She felt the rough edges beneath the burlap. She grabbed one sack and tugged the drawstrings open.

Yes, it was gold. By her estimation, the nuggets looked to be the same size as the one Wyatt had given her that day at the creek. And there were five sacks of them!

"Garnet?" Wyatt's voice. "I can see someone coming from town. I think it's Katy."

She couldn't speak. She could only stare at the sack in her hand, heavy and bulky, as Wyatt approached.

"Damn." His curse sounded like regret. "You found my stash of gold."

"This is what the thief was looking for," she choked. "You might have told me you hadn't lost your gold."

"I'm not certain that is what he wanted." Wyatt laid a hand on her shoulder.

"What else could he want? You have a fortune hidden away in the privy, of all places."

"It's not all my gold."

His confession startled her. She looked up at him, trying to measure the troubled shadows in his eyes. He lifted the burlap sack from her hands.

"Much of this was my brother's gold. This was his claim. He was killed in a violent struggle this past summer. From what I could tell someone tortured him trying to make him reveal where he hid his gold."

"And he never told?"

"Never."

Her hands trembled. Her knees felt weak. The safe winter world she'd dreamed of sharing with Wyatt faded. "Will the same thing happen to you?"

What would she do without him? The thought of losing him tore through her heart. She watched him replace the bag of gold with the others. Grim and silent, he nailed the board seat into place.

It occurred to her then that he'd lied. About his claim, about his gold. She could understand it; he didn't want anyone to know. What happened to his brother could happen to them. He wanted to protect her.

But he had told her so little about himself, about his past and his life. Were there other lies? What other secrets was he withholding?

Suddenly the future she'd envisioned didn't seem as certain or as bright.

"Is that why you left your respectable job? Because you were grieving over your brother's death?"

"Yes, it is."

"You inherited his claim."

"When he died, he no longer owned the deed. Someone took it from him before or after he died."

"How did you know where he hid the gold?"

Grief lined Wyatt's rugged face. "When we were boys, our father hid his savings from our mother in the outhouse. She spent every dime she got her hands on, so he hid it. It just seemed a logical place for Ben to hide his treasure, and I was right. When I came here, I found the gold. The gold he was murdered for." His gaze strayed to the road. "We'll talk later, when Katy is gone."

"Wyatt, I—"

"Later." Wyatt pressed a kiss to her forehead.

Her chest cracked, thinking of all he'd lost. Her love for him grew all the more, so big and bright and beautiful it took up all the room in her heart.

* * *

Wyatt headed for town as soon as the women were busy at their laundry. Garnet, her hair tied back with only a single blue ribbon and kneeling over a washboard, lifted a sudsy hand to wave him good-bye. Katy was busy changing the rinse water.

Garnet had offered a partnership to a prostitute and it surprised him, but what shocked him more was that she hadn't lost her temper when she'd discovered the gold. He'd hurt her, he knew. The nuggets hidden beneath the outhouse seat were only the tip of the lies he'd let her believe. How could he protect her from them? He could not live with the thought of hurting her.

Troubled, he arrived in town with too much on his mind. When he'd asked the judge for time off to solve his brother's murder, the job had seemed uncomplicated. Blend in. Find out everything he could about the fifty or so men who lived and prospected here. Narrow down the suspects. Arrest the killer. Until Garnet waltzed into his life.

"Wyatt," the saloon owner greeted from the road.

"Gus." Wyatt ripped his hat.

"Did you hear about Samuels?"

Samuels was the gunsmith. "No, why? I talked to him a few days ago."

"He's dead. Elmer Minks found him the next morning, shot once through the chest."

Just like Ben. "Was it a robbery?"

"Didn't look like it. Must have owed somebody money, that's what we're all figuring, anyway."

Except Wyatt had asked Samuels about the Winchester rifle, the one owned by the man who shot Garnet. Samuels had agreed to help him by checking through his records and making a list of men who had purchased or had repaired the same make of rifle.

Wyatt was sorry Samuels was dead. Because he had asked for Samuels's help. Well, that was another murder the killer would hang for, once he found him. And find him, Wyatt would. Now he was certain the man he sought was the same one who had shot Garnet that long ago night.

* * *

Wyatt shook the flap to Elmer Minks's tent. "I gotta talk to you, Minks." Then he looked inside. The place was empty. Only a wood pallet and the stove was left behind.

A neighboring tent's flap slung open. "Minks went to pick up his laundry from Miss Garnet."

It looked like he didn't intend to come back. He'd meant to pick up more tarpaper from Carson's store and try to get another look at Carson, but Wyatt ran down the street. He hoped he could make it in time.

* * *

Wyatt rounded the back corner of the cabin and heard Garnet's voice. "Mr. Minks, I can't possibly charge you the entire fee."

"But I—"

"Nonsense." She pressed a small gold nugget back into the miner's hand. "Those shirts were not ironed. It would go against my conscience to charge you so much."

"Yer mighty kind, Miss Garnet. You too, Miss Katy."

Wyatt puffed to a stop before the group. "Minks, I've got to talk to you."

The man's eyes widened. "I—I—" he stammered.

"Wyatt, don't terrify the poor man. He's just come to get his laundry. He's leaving town."

"I know." Wyatt nodded toward the road. "Minks, you had better come with me."

The man looked helplessly at the women, then shuffled out into the yard.

"Tell me what you saw when you found Samuels."

Minks blanched. "I didn't do it. Some folks started blamin' me right away. But I ain't never hurt no one all my life. I ain't a violent

165

man."

"I never said you were. Maybe the man who killed the gunsmith did it to keep him quiet. I think it's the same man who killed Ben."

"Ben was a mighty fine fella. Gave me a big fifty-dollar gold nugget one night when I got in over my head gamblin'. He saved my life, he did. I gave up poker after that. All thanks to him."

"I'm glad to know that." Wyatt's heart ached. Ben had been a good man; he didn't deserve having his life cut short. All Wyatt could do for his brother now was bring his killer to justice. "Did you see anything unusual in that shop? Something that would help?"

"Well, it was pert near thrashed. Someone dumped nearly everything on the floor."

"Tell me about the gunsmith's body."

"Burns. Like from a cigar. All over him." Minks choked.

Just like Ben's body. No doubt the killer was the same man. "Here's a few gold nuggets. The stage is still running south, even with the snow. Get as far away as you can."

"Will do."

Wyatt watched the miner scurry off, his rucksack slung over his shoulder. His suspects had been narrowed down to just two men. Two men in town who both used Winchester rifles, smoked cigars, and had the motive and opportunity to commit the murders.

By this time tomorrow, he would have Ben's killer.

* * *

Golda's feet felt heavy with every step closer to that awful Mr. Tanner's cabin. Even the wind blew against her, as if holding her back. Her stomach turned over at the thought of meeting her sister face-to-face after the things she'd said in the minister's parlor.

She saw Mr. Tanner saying good-bye to a prospector she recognized as neighboring her and Lance's tent. She wanted to avoid Mr. Tanner. Taking a sharp turn off the road, she headed around the side of the cabin. It looked different with the corner posts for the additional room and the new roof. It looked like paradise next to the filthy, cold tent Lance had forced her to live in.

"Golda!" Garnet's voice drew her up short. She wasn't prepared to see her sister looking so young, so beautiful.

That couldn't be Garnet. The wind ruffled her dark hair, tied at her nape and left to shiver down her back in a lustrous ebony ponytail. A beautiful dress hugged her slim form, and the tentative smile looked relaxed, even though it was troubled.

"Hi, Garnet," she managed, looking hard at the ground.

"This is Katy from town. I've offered her partnership in my cleaning business, since I needed help. I have too many clients for one person to handle." Garnet sounded nervous, but her voice was warm and gentle, not sharp, although echoes of hurt from the night in Virginia City remained. "I'm glad you stopped by. I have a wedding gift for you and Lance."

Golda followed her sister up the steps into the cabin and noticed the gold chain around her neck and the locket dangling between her breasts. A beautiful, expensive gold locket.

"Mr. Tanner must truly be fond of you." She choked the words out. "I'm sorry for the mean things I said."

Garnet pressed her lips together, tears pooling in her eyes. "It's forgotten. Here. I hope you like this."

Golda took the gift, wrapped loosely in brown paper. Inside were folds and folds of delicate lace.

"For your first home, when you and Lance save up enough money." Garnet sounded kind, not judgmental. "I'm sorry I ruined your wedding the way I did. I was wrong."

Hot, painful tears burned Golda's eyes. "I shouldn't have gotten married. Lance talks big, but he's lazy. He doesn't have long before the creek freezes up solid, and he spent all the money he had just getting us married. What am I going to do?"

"You're his wife, now, Golda. I can't tell you what to do anymore." Tender, those words.

"Our tent is always muddy and cold, and it isn't even paid off."

"Maybe I can offer you a job." Garnet lifted the coffeepot from the stove and poured four tin cups to the brim. "You wouldn't be a partner, since I offered that to Katy and she was here first."

"I understand."

Garnet set a half-eaten box of chocolates on the table, then dropped one in each cup. "I think we could arrange to have you and Lance rent Mr. Carson's cabin, but I would expect you to work hard. Both Katy and I do."

Shame bloomed in Golda's chest. "I know Garnet. I'm responsible for myself now. If I don't do a good day's work, you can fire me just like any employee."

"I'm glad you came back, Golda." Garnet smiled, and in that

smile shone a lifetime of love. "Let's take these outside to Wyatt and Katy. That wind out there is cold."

* * *

"Are you going to tell me what you said to scare Mr. Minks out of town?" Garnet asked as she slid a sawed board across the rafters.

"No." He pulled the board toward him. He looked good. Too good. Handsome and capable and stronger than any man she had ever known. The breeze tousled his dark hair. The strong, unforgiving line of his steel jaw softened with his smile. "If it were any of your business, I would have told you."

"So now you're keeping more secrets from me." She was only teasing. But his smile faded.

"I am. There are things you don't want to know about me. Believe me." He positioned a nail and drove it through the board with two blows from his hammer.

She pulled a nail from her apron pocket and drove it home in three. "Maybe I want to know."

Love wasn't an emotion he felt often or easily. But once he did, he loved with his entire heart. Therein lay the problem. His love for Garnet couldn't protect either one of them from a broken heart; it was inevitable. And his love for her couldn't change the man he was deep inside, a killer, a man who made his living with a gun.

He wasn't good enough for her, and he wasn't civilized enough. Not for such a woman of quality. How could he change his basic nature? He knew it was impossible, no matter how much he wanted to.

He pulled another board into place and they nailed it down, and then another. Garnet tipped her face to the sky, squinting across the landscape. She looked as if she belonged here, a vibrant woman in a wild, untamed country. The breeze shifted through her hair, and the sun glistened against it like light on silk. His fingers ached to wind through those midnight curls.

"Looks like we'll have the roof finished in no time. I smell more snow in the air." She didn't smile, and there was strain around her eyes. Strain he'd put there. "I can't wait to start putting in a real floor."

"Not many women can do carpentry work."

She squinted through the sunshine at him. "There was never enough money to hire out the work, so if the roof needed repairing or if a window leaked, I had to figure out how to fix it."

"You have your own money now, and a lot of it. What do you plan to do with it all?"

"This and that." She gave him a little mischievous grin. "What about you and all that gold?"

"Probably invest it, I guess. Maybe give part of it to a few charities. I think Ben would have liked that."

"You've given it a lot of thought." She fished in her apron pocket for a nail, bowing her chin.

"The gold isn't the only thing I misled you about." His confession felt like dust in his throat.

"So you've said." She hammered another nail into the board. "Are you going to tell me you're leaving town?"

"Something like that."

"Then what are we doing building a roof for this cabin?"

"Because I don't know if I can leave." He reached for another board and drew it snug across the width of the rafters before he dug for more nails. "I don't know how I can leave you."

"Oh, Wyatt." Great tears filled her eyes. She walked toward him on the new boards that creaked beneath her weight. Her lustrous hair billowed in the ever-present wind. "Whatever is wrong, you can tell me."

Could he? He had to. There was no choice.

"I'm not a prospector." The words squeezed past the tightness in his throat. "I'm a deputy marshal investigating a murder."

"Of your brother?"

"Yes." She was going to hate the deception. He braced himself, preparing for her rejection.

"You didn't trust me?" she whispered.

He swept off his hat and raked a hand through his hair. He tried not to look at her, didn't want to see the disappointment on her face. He stared hard at his boots. "I was just doing my job."

"You're a deputy marshal. As in a lawman. As in someone with a steady income."

Was that a smile he heard in her voice? The glowing sound of approval? "Yes. I have a dependable job and a regular paycheck."

"And you aren't a prospector and never want to be one, not even in your wildest fantasies."

"The only fantasies I have are of you." He shrugged. Maybe he shouldn't have admitted that.

"I should be furious," she said in a thin, trembling voice. She stood tall and willowy, the wind whipping her waist-length hair and snapping her dress. "You could have told me the truth, Wyatt. I know why you couldn't trust me because it was your job to deceive everyone. I also know you would never lie to me under any other circumstances."

"You have too much faith in me."

"Not enough. I loved you when I thought you were a man without a job, without permanence in his life. I can love you more knowing that you are the kind of man I can believe in, maybe even marry."

"I wouldn't say that, Garnet."

Her mouth opened, closed, opened, but she said nothing more. She looked as if she were afraid, as if she didn't know how to say what was in her heart.

She loved him. He could see it, the color of forever in her eyes.

But it couldn't be true. She just *thought* she loved him. Wyatt barricaded his heart before he became too vulnerable. Before he began to believe in such impossible dreams and tried to reach them again. And failed.

"You mean you don't love me enough to marry me?" Her hand flew to cover the locket hanging between her breasts, over her heart. Her chin trembled.

Damn, he'd made her cry. He reached out, but she backed away. She raised her chin, and he saw wetness on her cheeks. She was all tough determination, at least on the outside. He knew inside she was as soft and sweet as cookie dough.

"We should discuss our future." Pride firmed her chin. "I want to stay with you, Wyatt, but if you don't want me, then you should just say it. I know I tend to be a little pushy—"

"A little?" he questioned.

"And I tend to take over and run things—"

"I hadn't noticed."

"—only because I've never been able to lean on anyone for help. And I know I'm not pretty—"

"You're not." That made her meet his gaze. "You're beautiful to me. And you become more beautiful every time I look at you."

"Why don't you want me?" So much vulnerability shone in her eyes, soft as morning light, gentle as dawn.

"I never said that. I just said I couldn't marry you. I'm sorry. It's just not something I can do."

Heartbreak weighed down her voice and furrowed sad lines into her face. "You certainly aren't the only man who's had that opinion."

Was her heart breaking at the thought of not being with him?

Could it be? Could she honestly love him that much?

"I can't marry you unless you know the truth about me."

"I know everything that matters."

"I am a marshall. I use a gun for a living. I see parts of life I can't always forget when I come home for supper. Things that haunt me sometimes in the middle of the night."

"But you uphold the law. You make it safe for children to play in their yards and walk through the town to buy candy at the store. You arrest men who threaten people. You make it possible for towns to be peaceful, for families to live without fear."

"I also kill." He was good at what he did, and he would never work another job. Probably because he'd endured violence as a child and wanted to make damn sure no one else had to live that way. Sometimes, it meant pulling a trigger and ending a life. Too many times to count, enough that he didn't always sleep at night.

"You shoot criminals." Her certainty shone in her voice, true and unshakable.

Couldn't she see it made him unfit for her? She, with her proper life and standards and reputation awaiting her back home in New York.

A twig snapped behind him and Wyatt spun around, his heart slamming against his ribs.

"Don't make a move, Tanner, or I'll kill you, you nasty bastard." Barrett Carson stood in the yard, sunlight glinting off the cold metal of his Winchester rifle.

Damn. He should have been paying attention. But scolding himself wouldn't solve the problem. His hand inched toward his hip where his loaded revolver was holstered. "What do you want, Carson?"

"The gold. I want it *now*." The hissed threat sounded as final as death.

Wyatt felt Garnet's fear. Out of the corner of his eye, he saw her, pale and tense. Her jaw was clenched tight. She might be afraid, but she was angry, too. Just like he was.

His gun was strapped at his thigh, but Wyatt doubted he could draw in time. Carson looked to be pretty handy with that rifle. Especially with his finger on the trigger. So he lied. "The claim has panned out, just like the others along this creek. By spring this place will be a ghost town."

"You can't fool me, Tanner. The man who owned this claim before you took out bags and bags of gold. I didn't find any on him after he died, and that means you must have them. Show me where you stashed the nuggets."

"I'm going to have to climb down to do it."

"By all means." Carson edged closer. "But Garnet, you first. Tanner isn't going to try anything with a rifle pointed at you."

Damn. Wyatt hated watching her go, hated that Carson had a gun trained on her. He escorted her to the ladder and held the top steady while she descended. She gazed up at him, a question in her eyes. She trusted him to protect her, to know what to do. He liked that. Very much. He couldn't remember the last time anyone had that much faith in him.

"Throw down your gun belt first, Marshal Tanner." Carson laughed. "Yes, I figured out who you were. I saw your badge when I ripped apart your cabin."

"Then you've also figured out Ben was my brother." He reached for the buckle and tossed the gun to the ground.

"A lot of dead men have brothers. Don't worry, soon you'll be one of them."

Wyatt slid down the ladder and turned. He didn't see the rifle swing, but he did feel it slam into his jaw. Stars danced before his eyes, his vision dimmed. He fought it, but the pain dropped him to the ground.

"You shouldn't have let down your guard, Tanner." Carson laughed, standing over him in brand new boots, nicely tailored trousers, and a long coat that caught in the wind. "I know you've got the best paying claim this sorry little creek has ever seen. Probably better than half the digging down at Alder Creek."

"Probably." Blinking past the pain, Wyatt spied his gun, not even three feet away, lying in the mud. If he could just get to it, he knew he could take Carson.

"I noticed you haven't been spending much of that gold in town. A wise move, Tanner. I can only imagine what riches you've found."

"Let me up and I'll show you." *And put you in jail.*

Carson's eyes slitted. "Move slow, marshal. My finger is on the trigger and I can't wait to blow you away. Think of how I'll be able to comfort dear Miss Garnet when her lover is dead. She will have no one else to turn to."

"Mr. Carson! As if I am the kind of woman who would consort with a criminal."

Then, to Wyatt's amazement, Garnet slapped the murderer across the face with the flat of her hand. Carson stumbled, surprised.

Damn. He couldn't grab his revolver in time, so he snatched up the hammer and aimed. The handle struck Carson in the wrist. His gun fired wild as it flew from his grip.

"Oh, my gosh!" Garnet's distressed cry pierced through his mind, but already Wyatt was diving toward his holster.

He unsheathed the revolver and thumbed back the hammer. He pulled the trigger as Carson grabbed his rifle. He fired again when the Winchester's barrel flashed.

Pain drilled into Wyatt's head and the impact of the bullet flung him back against the side of the cabin. He knew he was hit, but one thing was certain. Carson had slumped to the ground with two bullets in his chest.

"Wyatt!" Garnet's voice, Garnet's hands at his face.

He shook the blood off his forehead. "Don't worry, the bullet just grazed me. I've been hurt worse."

"But you're bleeding." A handkerchief pressed against his brow, and the worry on her face made his heart stop.

She'd seen what he was up close. Witnessed how easy it was for him to pull a trigger. He stepped away from her, expecting her rejection, and knelt down beside Carson's body.

No pulse. This man had killed Ben, the only brother he had, but Wyatt never wanted to kill him. He'd only wanted the man tried for the crime and punished according to the law. Having to kill always left him hurting inside, sad for the loss of life, however undeserving.

"Wyatt?" Garnet's voice sounded so weak and far away. He turned to see the ashen hue on her face. That's when he knew for certain he had truly lost her. She'd seen how violent he was, what he was made of, and she couldn't stomach it.

Nothing he had endured, not even Ben's death, had ever hurt this much.

CHAPTER FIFTEEN

S now began to fall when Garnet stepped foot out of the Virginia City jail. Wyatt followed her outside, grim from delivering Barrett Carson's body and writing up his report. In all, the rich merchant's son was responsible for six murders, including Wyatt's brother.

"Do you think the stage will still be running?" she asked, gazing up at the silver-white sky. Tiny flakes fluttered into her eyes and tickled her face.

"Doesn't look like it will turn into a blizzard." He stuck his hands in his pockets and stared down the street. He felt so distant, he seemed like a different man.

But he wasn't. He was still her Wyatt, dependable and iron-strong. Although he no longer wore his miner's cotton shirt and Levi's. The tasteful black shirt and trousers, hat and boots set him apart from others on the street. Dangerous-looking men took a wide berth when they caught sight of him.

Winter was coming. She had run out of time. Before the mountain passes filled with snow, she had to make a decision. To leave, or to stay.

How could she stay? Wyatt didn't want to marry her. He had said those very words himself. It didn't matter if he was a miner or deputy marshal, he did not want her for anything more than a lover. He had a job. His lack of a stable profession was not keeping them apart.

He was. He feared he wasn't good enough for her. For her!

"Do you need me to recommend a hotel room?" he asked.

"No, I can find one on my own." She didn't need his help, she needed him.

Snow was accumulating on the brim of his hat and on the shoulders of his tailored black coat. His square jaw was set as if preparing to face an executioner, but his shadowed eyes revealed nothing. What was he feeling?

"Are you going to return to Stinking Creek?" she had to ask, had to know. "Or are you going home to your job?"

He bowed his chin and studied the ground. A lock of dark hair fell across his forehead. He looked rakish and respectable, dangerous and tame. Everything she could ever dream of in a man.

"I haven't decided yet." He leaned against the wall of the jail, his back to the wood. A muscle jumped in his clenched jaw. "I want to make certain you get on the stage all right. It's the least I can do for nearly getting you shot at twice by the same man."

"Mr. Carson was the man following Golda and me the first night we came to town?"

"As close as I can figure. Maybe he was worried you had some information about the gold since you were heading for my claim." He swept off his hat and raked his fingers through those thick, dark locks. "I almost failed you today. I let down my guard. He took advantage of it and caught me from behind. I could have gotten you killed."

"I'll try to forgive you." She teased him, the way she used to.

But there was no smile quirking his mouth, no flicker of humor in his eyes. "How can you ever forgive me? You've seen what I do for a living."

"What is wrong with being a deputy marshal? It's such an honorable profession."

"The men I hunt down are criminals, Garnet. Some criminals are animals, but others are just desperate men. Men in bad circumstances, who made a wrong choice or showed bad judgment. Many of them aren't so different from me."

She laid a hand on his arm. "It doesn't matter, Wyatt. I love you just the way you are. No matter what. And that will never change. You can bet on it."

She didn't understand, Wyatt knew. She was a sheltered proper woman, just like Amelia had been, raised without knowledge of the bad side of life, of human nature.

He loved Garnet. He wanted her to be his wife, to welcome him home after a tough day's work and fill him with her goodness, to hold him through the night and comfort him from those dreams he couldn't always shake.

He wanted it so much, he knew he had to face his fears. And let them go.

Garnet had watched him shoot Carson. She knew what he was. And yet she still loved him, saw the honor he tried to bring to his job, to his life.

Her hand touched his sleeve. "I am certain of my feelings for you, Wyatt. How do you feel about me?"

"I love you. More than anything."

He reached out and folded his hands over hers. Warm. Accepting. Filled with faith in her love, faith in their future together.

"We can do whatever you want, Garnet. We can stay in our cabin at the claim through the winter. Or we can head back to my house in Bannack, or—"

"You have a house?" she interrupted.

"A respectable job, a steady paycheck, and a mortgage. Am I stable enough for you?" Now he was teasing her.

She laughed, her chest filling with so much happiness she could hardly breathe. "I'll follow you anywhere."

"Then you'll have to marry me. Because if you think I'm going to sleep with you and live in sin without the benefit of holy matrimony, you are dead wrong."

"But I'm a free spirit now. I've learned to drink alcohol and play poker and pan for gold."

"Stop teasing and kiss me."

His mouth covered hers with a passionate brush of heat and lips. Sheer joy swelled in her heart. She wrapped her arms tightly around his broad, iron-strong shoulders. There was no greater treasure in all of Montana Territory. And he was hers.

An Excerpt from

The Rancher's Return

CHAPTER ONE

"No!" Nettie felt the skin prickle on the back of her neck despite the heat and the sun. In a flash she halted the wagon, harnesses jangling, and hauled her two-and-a-half-year-old son onto her lap, shielding him from the sight before them.

She recognized her neighbor, Jake Beckman, his big frame silhouetted by the bright red-orange disk of the harsh sun, his head bare. Nettie watched in horror as he drew his strong leg backward, his gaze trained on a downed man in the middle of the road, and slammed his boot into the fallen man's midsection with all of his oxlike strength.

"Stop it!" she demanded. "Stop this right now."

Jake jerked his gaze to her. Several other men stepped into view on the rise above, dark figures outlined by the bright glare of the sun and the deep cloudless blue of the sky.

"This ain't none of your business, Nettie." Jake mopped the sweat from his brow with a swipe of his arm. "Come on, boys, let's get this worthless piece of crap off the road so the lady can pass."

Nettie's ears burned at the venom in Jake's voice. She felt her spine straighten with the need to remind him of her and her son's sensibilities, but now her gaze focused on the man lying so still on the ground. He was dirty, hatless, his shirt torn. Yet even with his back to her, something skidded through Nettie's nerves. Like fear. Like the time she heard the gunshot and knew her husband was dead.

One of the men on the rise dragged the man from the road. "Come on, Nettie," Jake instructed her. "Pass on by."

Silence roared through her ears with the strength and speed of a train so that suddenly, she knew. She *knew*. The man who lay hurt and bleeding and broken was the same man who had killed her husband.

"Come on, Nettie," Jake's voice called her forward.

It was as if the great expanse of the sky was her heart. Unable to feel, Nettie shook the reins, aware of Sam's wide-eyed fear as he cuddled against her on the seat and Old Bessie's protesting groans as they lumbered up the side of the slope. The wooden slats of the wagon rattled. One wheel squeaked. Nettie stared at the passing patch of earth between the tongue of the wagon and the horses' tails.

"Just go on to town," Jake said as she approached. "We'll be along in a few minutes." He spoke casually of the funeral and of his delay as if he were about to tie up his horse or run an errand, not beat a man to death.

Memory slammed through her head with lightning speed. She remembered the threats, two years before, and how her neighbors had taken a stand behind her. Jake had threatened to kill the man if he ever showed his face in the county again.

Nettie pulled the reins hard. Bessie squealed in protest at the pressure on her mouth, but it was a distant sound compared to the heartbeat so loud in her ears. Nettie turned to study the man in the dust. Blood ran from his brow and mouth. His leg lay at a strange angle.

"You men ought to be ashamed of yourselves," Netie chided as if she were scolding Sam for a misdeed. She left the child on the seat and hopped down from the wagon. Five men stared at her, their eyes dark, their mouths curled into frowns.

Anger. It burned in her breast as fiercely as the sun overhead. It emboldened her now as she halted before the strong, burly men. Men she knew. Men capable of violence. Her hands trembled, but she didn't think of it now. She knelt down next to the man on the ground.

Hank Callahan opened one eye as the woman's shadow threw relief over his hammering body. He had heard Jake Beckman speaking to a woman. He had heard a wagon stop, a horse's complaint, and a woman speak.

Nettie Pickering gazed down at him with concern in her wide brown eyes. Green threads wove through those dark irises like grass on the plain. He opened his mouth to tell her to go, to leave him be, but it only roused up more pain. Pain struck through every piece of him with the force of an ax and it didn't stop.

She was dressed for a funeral. A black straw hat shaded her soft oval face from the sun, and a dusty black dress hugged her from chin to wrist. Ebony fabric skirted her as she knelt, leaning closer, brushing at the cut above his eye with the lightest touch of her small hand.

The ground beside his head shook with little earthquakes. A small tow-haired child grabbed Nettie's arm. Concern frowned across the boy's brow as he leaned close. "Mama, why's he got so many ows?" he asked.

Nettie's soft mouth compressed into a tight line. Hank watched as she brushed a lock of flyaway hair from the boy's innocent eyes. "Sam, tell me why you aren't waiting in the wagon."

The boy shrugged, and Hank drew in a tentative, painful breath as the boy scampered away. Nettie moved from his side, the crisp black fabric rustling around her. Hank watched her slender body rise with a spine-straight dignity. The sun glared around her and heat burned right into the pain in his guts, doubling it.

A boot nudged him hard in his tender right side. Hank snapped open his eyes to stare up at a black-shirted man, who was also dressed for the funeral. Harv Wheaton nudged him hard with his pointed boot's toe. "You're a dead man, son."

Hank swallowed. He understood the quiet certainty in the man's frank statement. Hank was a murderer in many men's eyes, even his own. When the men he'd called neighbors ran him out of town that dark night over two years ago, Hank knew he could never come back. But here he was.

A shadow slipped across him, blocking out the harsh burn of the sun like cold water. He could smell the cinnamon soap scent of her and hear the rustle of her skirts as Nettie knelt beside him again.

"Jake, Harv, Thomas, help me get him into the wagon." Her voice sounded as firm as the earth beneath his head.

"Now, Nettie. This here is none of your business." Jake's boot stopped within kicking distance. Hank knew the big man's placating voice would urge her away, insist that she continue on her journey to town, and leave them to finish this. It was what Hank expected.

But Nettie stood up, the rock-hard confidence in her voice unmistakable. "This man needs a doctor."

"This man needs a hanging," Harv argued.

"If you don't lift him into the back of my wagon, then I'll do it myself."

Hank felt a small hand catch up each of his wrists and begin pulling him across the rocky, rough earth. Pointed stones bit into his back. His head banged with each small dip and rise.

His leg felt as if someone were ripping it out of his knee joint. Darkness buzzed in Hank's brain until he was hardly aware of the beating sun and the abuse of the ground upon his body. He couldn't even hear the men arguing.

Then a white blast of pain careened through his body as several rough hands ripped him from the ground and tossed him into the back of a wagon.

Pain battered him until he welcomed the comforting blackness.

"You're asking for trouble, Nettie," Jake Beckman cautioned her. "He killed your husband."

"I know that." Nettie's grip on the reins tightened. She couldn't explain her actions, but she knew in her heart she'd done the right thing. "If I had allowed you to beat Hank Callahan to death, then you wouldn't be any better than a murderer."

She clamped her mouth shut She didn't owe Jake Beckman any more of an explanation than that. If she closed her eyes she could still see his vicious and powerful kick to a barely conscious man unable to fight back. Her chest filled with angry sparks of rage.

"Mama." Sam stood up in the wagon bed behind her, his little fingers gripping the wooden seat back. "The man's bleedin'."

"I know, tiger. He's hurt." She unclenched her jaw enough to speak. "Now come sit back down beside me.

"Justice isn't murder, Nettie," Jake spoke with unfailing certainty.

She closed her eyes, counted to ten. For a day that had begun as uneventful as any, her troubles had sorely increased. A funeral to attend. Jake Beckman hovering over her. Now Hank Callahan beaten and vomiting in the back of her old wagon.

Nettie glanced over her shoulder. Blood-tinged spittle clung to the beaten man's lips and chin. A wet patch had darkened the boards, but most of it had already dripped between the slats.

She reached into one skirt pocket and handed Sam a handkerchief. "Can you be a big boy and wipe off his mouth for Mama?"

"Okay." Sam took the piece of plaid cloth and crawled the handful of inches to Hank's head. Nettie watched as he wiped the man's mouth hard. Triumphant, he grinned up at his mother.

"Good boy," she said, and Sam was satisfied.

"That murderer oughtn't be near your boy," Jake pointed out, his hard-featured face harsh beneath the dark brim of his hat.

That hard anger tightened like a fist inside Nettie's chest. "I know you've been a wonderful neighbor and friend to me since Richard's death, but I don't like this. You did this to him, Jake, and I'll expect you and the men to pay the doctor's bill."

The man riding beside her wagon shook his head. "You're too kind for your own damn good, Nettie. I don't care if you like it or not, I'm not leaving you alone with a known murderer. We'll get him to town, and that will be the end of your worries."

Nettie sighed. "Today is Mr. Callahan's funeral. Don't you realize Hank came to town to see his father buried? Surely you could have left him alone."

Jake spat a wad of tobacco juice away from the wagon. "I've known you a long time, Nettie. You won't marry me and you won't marry anyone else around here that's tryin' to help you. Now you just gotta trust that a man knows how to handle this."

Nettie opened her mouth, her angry protest already a string of words in her throat, but she hesitated. She did not agree with Jake Beckman, but he had been more than a good neighbor to her. She couldn't afford to anger him even if she would never agree with his way of thinking.

She snapped her mouth shut, her jaw muscles aching.

"Mama." Sam grabbed the board behind her and leaned into her ear. "Looky."

Nettie glanced over her shoulder past the sun-blond head of her young son to the man lying prostrate on her wagon floor. His strong, masculine body trembled, shivering as if he were in a frigid wind.

She pulled the horses to a stop, set the brake because of the incline, and hopped over the wagon seat. Her skirts fell around her ankles as she hurried to the man's side.

He looked like death. A bright red cut slashed the skin above his left eyebrow and wet blood trailed down the side of his pasty white face. Dark eyelashes fanned the bruises of his eyes; the soft, sensual line of his mouth was swollen in several places, and the split skin bled.

"He got lots of owies." Sam stared down at the injured man.

"Yes, he does." Nettie sighed. "Where is your hat? Put on your hat so you don't get sunburned."

While Sam grabbed up his small hat made just like Jake's, Nettie grabbed a folded blanket from beneath the seat and tucked it around the shivering man. In her heart, she feared he was close to death. Dead for nothing more than coming home to his father's funeral.

Jake had pulled his horse up to the wagon bed, and his shadow fell across Nettie's feet. The man's dark eyes were unreadable beneath the brim of his hat, and she frowned at him, meeting his gaze for a second longer than necessary.

"I'm sorry, Nettie." His voice came gruff but not apologetic.

She said nothing. What was there to say? She condemned what he'd done to this man. She condemned violence of any sort. Perhaps it was because her father's love for whiskey had driven him to abuse his wife and his family and to land him in jail for brawling in the streets. Perhaps it was simply because striking someone never solved one problem that she could see. Either way, Nettie snatched up Sam's hand in her own and lifted him gently over the back of the seat.

"Sit still and watch for gophers," she instructed the boy as she climbed over the boards herself, careful of her skirts. "I bet you can find two or three before we get to town."

With Sam busy, there were no more innocent questions begging to be answered. Jake rode silently beside the wagon. And Nettie settled into her own thoughts, troubled, afraid the man in the back would die before they reached town.

Walla Walla boomed dirty and noisy as Nettie carefully negotiated the main street. Tall brick-and-wood buildings faced her, and movement swirled around her. Shoppers jammed the boardwalks. Horses and buggies stood tethered. Freight wagons crammed the streets, and Nettie waited impatiently until she could nudge around the slow-moving traffic and off the main street.

She pulled up before a tidy white building and told Jake to find someone inside. Sam chattered on about what he'd seen, and Nettie tried to answer him as she glanced at their passenger in the back. The shivering had ceased. He lay like a corpse buried beneath the dark wool blanket. Nettie distracted Sam, her heart heavy, and lifted him down from the wagon.

The grass was cool in the dappled shade, and Nettie sent the boy to pick clover. She watched his gentle footfalls and his little-boy innocence with a tight throat. He would grow up to be gentle like his father, wouldn't he? Troubled, she remembered Jake's behavior today and shivered.

At least the question that had been troubling her for three weeks was answered. She would not marry him.

A serious, solid man wearing dark clothes and spectacles burst out into the sunlight and raced toward the back of the wagon. Nettie wanted to help, but feared there was nothing she could do. She was not a nurse. She could not breathe life back into Hank Callahan if he was dead. She could only pray that he was still alive, or pray for the state of his soul.

"Mama?" Sam held up a fistful of white-and-brown clover flowers.

She smiled at him. She could protect her son. Kneeling down, Nettie accepted the flowers.

Sam stared, worry deep in his brow, watching as the doctor and Jake hauled Hank out of the wagon.

She was told by the doctor to wait. She pulled out Richard's pocket watch from her reticule and studied the time. Although she'd arrived plenty early for the funeral, Nettie had been counting on running errands before the service. She thought of the horses, hot and thirsty, and wandered outside hoping to find a water trough.

There wasn't one close. She boosted Sam onto Emmanuel's broad back. The placid horse stood patiently in his harness while the boy squirmed excitedly. Nettie placed one hand on his leg and led the horses into the dappled, pleasant shade. Out of the direct sunlight, they would be cooler.

"Nettie." Jake strode toward her, his eyes dark. A ring of sweat gathered below the band of his hat, matting his hair and beading along his brow. "Doc says it'll be a long wait. Why don't you go on over to the funeral. I got me a few errands to run, but I'd be happy to escort you."

Nettie stared at him, unable to speak. She'd known this man for years. He'd been a friendly neighbor when Richard lived, a helpful neighbor after Richard died. A friend whenever she needed one. Now, in the span of hours, he'd become a stranger to her.

"I want your word there will be no more violence against that man in there." Nettie swallowed, her throat dry and raw. "Promise me, Jake."

She watched him set his square jaw and some glimmer of doubt twisted through her like a snake in the tall bunchgrass. She couldn't see what he intended to do. She wasn't sure she could trust what he would do.

"I can't trust a man who'd lie to me."

The stiffness in his strong shoulders ebbed. "You have my word. I'll see that he's left alone."

Nettie studied him, weighing the sincerity of his tone against the steady firmness of his eyes. "Is that the truth?"

Jake sighed. "It's the truth."

Nettie pulled Sam down and balanced him on her hip. He was heavy to hold, but she clung to him despite the heat. "I have errands of my own," she told him plainly as she set her son on the wagon floor. "I'll look for you at the funeral."

Jake tipped his hat, clearly displeased with her. With her stomach so twisted up in knots, Nettie didn't care how unhappy he was or what he thought of her for not harboring the same hateful vengeance he did. She only hoped she could trust him to keep to his word. She only hoped Hank Callahan would recover, leave town, and never return.

Now Available

ABOUT THE AUTHOR

Jillian Hart makes her home in Washington State, where she has lived most of her life. When Jillian is not writing away on her next book, she can be found reading, going to lunch with friends and spending quiet evenings at home with her family.

26825249R00110

Made in the USA
Lexington, KY
17 October 2013